"The Club"

By

"I. B. Cuffman"

The Club

Copyright 2007
By
Rich B. Publishing

Published in 2007

Book design by
Rich B. Publishing
P. O. Box 404
Nichols, South Carolina
29581

E-mail--RichBPublishing@aol.com

Published in the United States

ISBN---987-0-6151-5124-3

Introduction

Bryan Wescott—a young handsome accountant—Sally Saunders a lovely young receptionist that loves tight bondage, put them together in a nowhere job and looking to move ahead, and you have the makings for an interesting set of events. Their relationship ends and it sends Bryan on a quest to become a consultant, for a financial firm. He moves across country to find three women that become a major part of his new life. Kim his angel, Kelly, and Peggy the undercover agents, they all love the world of BDSM and regularly play. The agents are there to uncover a white slave ring that has kidnapped one young beautiful woman a month, for the last 18 months. They know that the East Coast is the staging ground for transportation of these women to their new owners, and Bryan is thrust into the middle of the investigation. Tight bondage, suspension in various forms, BDSM at its best, fill the investigation. Submissive women, sex, intrigue, violence, love, and desire, led Bryan on a quest for the future, at "The Club."

Table of Contents

Chapter 1   **The Date**   *Page 1*

Chapter 2   **The Cabin**   *Page 23*

Chapter 3   **The New Toy**   *Page 46*

Chapter 4   **The Interview**   *Page 61*

Chapter 5   **The Castaway Club**   *Page 74*

Chapter 6   **Nick's Social**   *Page 88*

Chapter 7   **The New Clients**   *Page 107*

Chapter 8   **Level 2**   *Page 120*

Chapter 9   Level 3   *Page 136*

Chapter 10   **The Ring Harness**   *Page 157*

Chapter 11   **The Reversal**   *Page 170*

Chapter 12   **The Kidnapping**   *Page 184*

Chapter 13   **Kelly's Torment**   *Page 199*

Chapter 14   **The Rescue**   *Page 215*

The Date (Chapter 1)

His voice was strong and demanding; there was no room for discussion when he told her to put her hands together in front of her. Sally Ford felt the cold metal ring of the handcuff encircle her left wrist and heard the sharp snap of the lock. Then her right wrist felt the same hard unyielding steel, and again, the sharp snap of the lock. It flashed through her mind that letting Bryan handcuff her like this might not be the right thing to do, at least not on the first date—although inviting herself to his apartment for supper and a movie had been almost an invitation for him to take advantage.

Holding her arm, he led her across the room to the queen-size bed and told her to lie down with her hands and arms stretched over her head. An eerie shiver of desire went through her body at his dominating directions—a desire she had felt in the past, to reach that beautiful, sensual dimension of submission. He tied a three-quarter-inch cord to the short length of chain separating her handcuffs and secured it to the middle headboard rail of the bed.

Her firm breasts stood at attention, jutting from her chest like majestic erotic mountains, their tight areolas and thick extended nipples hard and remarkably sensitive. There was no physical pain at this time, only an amazing sensation of anticipation as she waited for what she hoped would be sexual rapture. She was letting go of control and she knew it.

Her eyes focused on Bryan as he reached into his large black gym bag, removed a pair of strong-looking black leather cuffs, and held them up for her to see. The corner of her mouth turned up in a smile, offering a concession that she soon would be completely helpless. "Bryan," she said, "the scent of the leather is so intoxicating, it makes me so wet."

He did not reply, but fastened a leather shackle to each of her ankles, then tested the tightness by pulling on them. That innate, indefensible emotion Sally remembered from her college days grew inside her with his steady tug on each strap. She was like a dedicated student in a classroom, waiting for her teacher to guide her into a new adventure in absolute submission.

He spread her long, luscious legs and secured the cuffs' shining steel rings to the corner posts of the bed. She was a little amused when she noticed his pleasure at the sight of her exquisite slit and the opening to her womanhood.

"Sir?" she asked, slightly raising her pussy off the bed, "Is this better?"

"My precious Sally, you're just a little slut! I'm very surprised at you. I never thought you'd be this way."

It was easy to see that he knew very little about her. Sally's demeanor at the office never revealed that she had a love for bondage and discipline, but her first experience mixing bondage and sex had happened in her senior year of college. Since then, she had never forgotten that amazing passion of release—her body and mind compelled to let go and have someone else take control.

"You shouldn't call me a slut," she said without thinking. "I don't do this with everybody, you know."

He stood there scrutinizing her callous remark. "I guess you mean that to be a slut, you have to be tied up and have sex with a lot of different people?"

"Something like that." Her voice quivered as she tried to be persuasive.

"Well, I'm not sure about that, but what I'm sure of is that there's way too much hair around that incredible slit of yours. I think I might just have to shave that off."

There was some danger involved in what he proposed. She stared at him, intensely turned on and afraid at the same time. He just might do it. "Are you for real?" she asked, her voice rose a little higher with excitement. "You're not *really* gonna do that, are you?" She struggled in her bonds, but no effort could change her position on the bed. He could do anything, and she was powerless to stop him even if she wanted to.

"In due time, in due time, sweetheart."

It was agonizing for her to watch him smirk and gaze at her pubic hair and naked body, but it must have inspired him, for she could feel his desire and see it in his face. "I'll be right back," he said.

She watched his lean, athletic body as he crossed the dimly lit bedroom. The growing bulge in his shorts suggested his desire was genuine.

She felt wetter just thinking he might put that tool of his inside her hot pussy.

He left her alone to contemplate her destiny for what seemed like hours, listening to her own breathing and her heart beating like some tribal drum. Actually, only a few minutes had passed when he came back with soap, a bowl of water, a washcloth, and a razor. He obviously meant to take advantage of this opportunity to shave a helpless woman's pussy.

"Oh my! You're for real, aren't you?" Sally gasped, her eyes taking in the sight of the shaving utensils. "It's been a long time since I've been shaved down there." She struggled in her well-secured restraints.

He saw her reaction, and a devilish smile appeared at the corners of his mouth. "I don't think you have much choice in this then, do you?" He could tell she was nervous, but he was in complete control and she had lost hers. She was his toy for him to play with in any way he wanted.

"I guess not," she replied, her voice a little defiant, as if it was no big deal. He knew better. She swallowed hard and braced herself for his first contact, wondering if he noticed the beads of sweat that were trickling down her face. He dipped the washcloth in the bowl of water and applied it to her pussy to soften the hair.

"*Damn*, that's cold! You're using *ice water*?" she squealed, trying to pull her head up from the bed.

"That's right," he announced as if she had answered the secret question of the day.

"Would you like to see the ice cubes?"

She knew it was no use to continue struggling; the straps were too tight, and when she felt the cold steel of the razor touch her wet slit, she thought it might be wise to lie as still as possible.

A short time later, after several careful strokes, he put the razor down and tenderly spread the folds of her pussy to make sure no hair was missed. "Not bad," he said. That's not bad at all, and would you believe, not a hair in sight?"

She breathed a sigh of relief that he had not hurt her during the deliciously torturous event. His strong sensitive hands felt phenomenal on her sex, but her body yearned for more. "I'm glad you didn't cut me," she said gratefully.

He did not answer as he returned to his bag of destiny and retrieved a black leather riding crop, about eighteen inches long, with a wide flap end— a mincing little thing that fit his hand perfectly. He snapped it and she heard it whistle through the air.

"Do you know what this is?" Bryan asked, holding the whip in front of her. He lightly grazed her nipples with its tip to tease her. A whip was something new to her, and she shuddered at the light touch. She could tell he was enjoying her reactions to this little show.

"Yes, it's an English riding crop." She licked her lips, eagerly anticipating the thrill of pain and pleasure that she'd hoped for. She wondered where he would land the first blow.

"Do you know what I'm gonna do with it?" he asked.

"Yes, sir." Her voice quivered again. "You're going to whip me with it."

"Have you ever been whipped before?" He lightly tapped the palm of his left hand with the whip.

"No, sir!" she said quickly. "I've never had a whip used on me, but I was spanked as a child when I was a bad little girl. It wasn't so bad—my parents never knew that I enjoyed it. As an adult, I've only read about it and seen a few movies. They say it hurts like hell, but the pleasure is much more intense than the pain. Remember the movie you showed me earlier?"

"Yes, I remember the movie. I thought it might have been too much for you when you left the way you did," he said.

She made no comment.

"Well, in any case," he said, "I think it's time we found out if the pain and pleasure thing is true."

Sally's body tensed as she grabbed the headboard rails on the bed for support.

"First though, if this is as painful as you say it might be, I don't want the neighbors to hear any loud noise."

He put the whip on her stomach so she could get a better look at it while he opened his bag of tricks. Her gaze was fixed on the whip; the sensation of the leather on her skin was intensely sensual. She relaxed her hands a bit until he showed her the bright red ball gag with its leather strap and buckle.

"Open up!" he ordered.

Sally stared at the red ball. "Bryan, you know, I didn't think this was on tonight's menu," she said hesitantly. She knew she would comply, but she was still a little anxious.

He just waited with the gag in his hand. Finally, she swallowed hard and obediently opened her mouth to take the gag. The rigid ball eased into place beyond her front teeth, and he tightly buckled the soft leather strap behind her head.

The gag made her feel even more incredibly helpless, giving her only a slight chance to make some inaudible sound. She wanted to tell Bryan how excited she felt lying helpless in front of him. The control he had over her was so powerful, but it was obvious that his power over her was still increasing.

"Let's see, how about fifty strokes on that pretty slit of yours? After taking off all that hair, I bet it's sensitive as hell. Don't worry," he said, petting her pussy. "I'll take my time, it won't be so bad, and who knows?" He grinned. "You might enjoy it."

She gripped the bed rails tightly again as she tried to prepare her body for the whip. The first stroke sent an agonizingly searing pain into her sex. It was a good thing she had the gag in her mouth; her scream could have woken the dead. "*Nooouhh!*" It was the only sound the gag would permit. Her body stiffened and shook at the same time. She arched her back and her head sank into the pillow. "*Nooouhh!*" The second stroke produced the same results.

As Bryan watched her body's reactions to the whip, the earlier bulge in his shorts became a full erection. More strokes followed, and sweat began to appear on Sally's chest. Drool began to ooze out of her mouth and down her chin from the corner of the gag. After twenty-five strokes on her sensitive pussy, he stopped.

"I just love it when my women sweat," he said. "It adds a great deal to the sex, don't you think?" Sally was so wrapped up in the fire of the whip that she never heard him, and couldn't answer if she wanted to.

He rested the whip on her stomach again and licked the sweat from her chest and the side of her face, like an African lion feasting on its fallen prey. "Man that tastes good!"

. Her breasts were heaving up and down with her labored breathing. This was far beyond her previous experiences of just being tied and having sex. She was in uncharted waters, dealing with exquisite pleasure and pain at the same time. He made a game of licking the sweat from her breasts between breaths, stopping to kiss each of her nipples and nip at them with his teeth.

"A woman's beauty only increases when she's in bondage," he continued. "I love to watch her struggle in the ropes and her efforts to escape. I guess you have to be a guy to appreciate that." Even though he had just whipped her, his soft voice seemed reassuring and inspiring.

His eyes moved from her breasts back to her pussy. Her clit was red from the whip and pulsating with each breath she took. It seemed her pussy had a mind of its own; it wanted more whipping, and she could say nothing about it. "I wonder if your pussy is as wet as it looks," he said as he gazed upon her nakedness.

She felt the hardness of his tongue lightly touch her clit and slide down into the depths of her moist opening, and relinquished all rights to any control she thought she might have had. He continued to lick around the edges of her slit, sending fiery shivers through her body.

"*Umm! Umm!*" She closed her eyes and bit into the gag. His tongue was everywhere, instinctively exploring all the regions of her sex. With all her effort, she tried to move her pussy closer to his mouth. Her bondage prevented much movement, but it was enough to let him know she was in fantasy heaven.

"Just as I expected, it's like a small river down there. *Man*, that's good!" he said, savoring the nectar of her love juices. He picked up the whip again. "If you remember, my lovely slave, I told you fifty and I'm only halfway there."

Sally clutched the bed rails again; it gave her some sense of security. She closed her eyes and waited for his glorious whip. The next twenty-five were just like the first. Her pussy cried from the pain of the whip, but at the same time, her body yearned for more. It was pure joy for her to please this man in any way she could.

She was concentrating so hard on each stroke and the orgasm she was about to have that it surprised her when he dropped the whip and moved away from the bed. She watched him cross the room to the closet and fumble around for a few seconds.

When he returned, she wondered if his imagination had taken leave of his senses. *What the hell is that damn broom handle for?* She thought. With the gag still compressed tightly in her mouth, she was unable to scream. Her nerves were on edge and her mind was racing. She prayed that whatever he did wouldn't really hurt her.

With a large piece of duct tape, he secured the broom handle to the bed rails behind Sally's hands. She craned her head back, trying to see what he was doing, but all she saw was the handle standing like a flagpole behind her head.

He tied one end of a three-quarter-inch rope to the handle and attached the other end to the ceiling fan over the bed. She was glad the fan was off. Then he looped a second piece of rope over that rope, leaving the ends just above her breasts, with one end noticeably shorter than the other. He attached small metal clips to the ends of the rope and pinched each nipple with his fingers, lightly at first, then increasing the pressure. Her nipples were already rock-hard, but this made them even more sensitive.

Clothespins were next. When he clamped one to her right nipple, a muffled cry escaped the gag. "*Shhhooott!*" Her head sank into the pillow, causing her to arch her back. "*Shhhooott!*" She let out another cry as he clamped her left nipple. She was breathing hard again, causing her breasts and nipples to jut upward.

Two pieces of string came next. He looped one piece over the right clothespin, then pulled the string tight around her nipple. She arched her back again and closed her eyes at the intense pain of the string. He did the same to the left nipple and then attached both strings to the long rope end that hung just above her breasts. There was very little play in the string.

Sally opened her eyes again and saw him reach back into his bag. She almost lost it when she saw him produce an odd, heavy-looking weight; it reminded her of a large banana with a ring attached to one end. She couldn't look away from the weight as he smiled at her. She wanted to tell him there were no way her breasts and nipples could handle it, but the gag prevented that.

"It's only two pounds," he said as if it were nothing at all. "I'm quite sure you can handle this." He attached the weight to the short end of rope and eased it down.

"*Ahaaaa! Ahaaaa!*" she cried out at the pain in her nipples and breasts as the weight stretched them skyward. She clenched her fists and tried to arch her back. She could barely maintain control of her emotions from the strain, not to mention the pain. She couldn't do anything but lie there and endure, and he wasn't through yet.

Her eyes closed again from the exquisite pain and pleasure her body was undergoing, and she didn't see him take another item from his bag.

"Open your eyes," he told her and waited for her to focus on his new toy.

It was an egg-shaped vibrator with a thin cord attached to a small control box. With his fingers, he separated her pussy lips. She relaxed her inner muscles as he inserted the egg just inside her vagina.

He pulled off a piece of duct tape from a roll he had on the nightstand. "This will keep it in place," he said, taping the egg inside her pussy. "I'm quite sure this will give you some pleasure at first, but let's just see how long it can stay there." He switched the vibrator on, sat back on the bed, and watched.

Her body jerked and shivered at the same time. He could see her breasts and nipples following suit, and with all that weight, it was a remarkable sight. Her bondage restricted her movements, but she could move enough for him to witness the beginning of an orgasm. The show continued for several minutes.

"I'm going to get another beer," he told her. "Enjoy and I'll be back soon."

The look on her face was priceless. *"YORE OT Eving E AST A!"* Her words were muffled by the gag, but he was still able to understand what she said. The gag was definitely doing its job.

"Yes, I'm leaving for a few minutes. Don't worry, I'll be back." He turned off the light and closed the door as he left the room.

In the living room, Bryan sat down at his computer with a beer in hand. He turned it on, and as it came to life, he reflected back on the day's events and what was unfolding in front of him.

Sally had reminded him of another young and beautiful woman he met one night at a local college hangout. He had just finished his night class and was heading home when he decided to stop for a beer. He was sitting in a small booth drinking his suds when this brown-eyed beauty approached his table and asked if she could join him.

"Of course," he said. He walked her home, and their relationship started that night. When they were undressing to get into bed, she produced a rope and wanted him to tie her up before they had sex. Bryan was surprised at her request, but with a devil in his eye, followed her instructions.

From that point on, Bryan's life changed in the bedroom. She stirred things in him that he had yearned to experience at an earlier age. It was the start of his training in becoming a sadist. Each time they were together, she taught him the fine art of bondage, discipline, and torture—choosing to desire the pain in order to achieve the pleasure it brings. Of course that ended when he finished college and moved away.

He and Sally had watched a great DVD movie about cops and robbers; it was more about robbers than about cops. The movie might have been too much for her, though, since it included a woman being kidnapped, bondage, and rape. When she got up and left so suddenly, he didn't know what to say. He was surprised that she'd come back.

Bryan had finished college about two years prior and had taken a job with Samuel's Accounting. He wanted to make good, and he had achieved some success, but the job wasn't what he had hoped it would be. He could see himself twenty-five years from now still doing the same job, and that was not a good thing.

Earlier that afternoon, he had completed his work and was looking out of his office window, watching the sun slipping behind the mountains. The leaves of the young oak tree just outside his window were rustling in a light breeze when he heard a faint tap on his office door.

It was Mr. Samuel's' cute and sexy little secretary, Sally Ford. As always, she was dressed in a business suit; always the perfect lady, not showing off her womanly figure, but he knew there was a beautiful woman in there somewhere.

"Sorry to bother you," she said. "I'm leaving, and you and I are the only ones left, so can you please make sure all the lights are out and the door is locked when you leave?"

"Of course. Don't worry; I'll take care of it." He smiled at her. "You know, it's so frustrating. I just don't understand how people can start a business and have no clue about keeping records! I've had four clients this week and it just amazes me."

Sally nodded. "I know what you mean. All of our accountants have said the same thing."

Bryan settled back in his chair, folding his hands behind his head. "For me, I'm gonna get a six-pack, go home, and relax. What about you, any big plans for the weekend?"

"Well—" She hesitated. "I have a business partner. Sara is her name."

"A business partner?" he asked.

"That's right. She and I want to buy a country and western bar in the next state. They bring in bands, and the dance floor is out of this world! Sara's an accountant like you, and she's been doing the books and says the owner has done well. We were going to go see the place again this weekend, but she can't go. Some boyfriend problem or something."

"Well, that sounds great!" Bryan said. "I'd be glad to look at your books if you like—maybe I can offer some kind of opinion. I've always wanted to do consulting work, and this might be good practice."

Sally knew he was a good accountant, not to mention attractive. She'd had her eye on him for a long time, but she had to be careful about relationships at work. Maybe this was an opportunity for her to get to know him better.

"Why not?" A smile emerged on her face. "I'll let Sara know we have a great consultant ready to help us in our charge to success." She dropped her head a bit, not sure if she should say anything else, but then looked at Bryan again. "Since Sara can't go this weekend, I'm not gonna go either. How would you like to get something to eat later?"

He considered her question for a few seconds. Sally had always been a model employee in the office and never socialized with any of the other staff. This was something new. *She opened a door, so why not see where it leads?*

"A buddy of mine gave me a movie to watch and said it was very interesting," he said. "Why don't you bring a pizza over? I'll pick up some beer and we can have supper at my place, what do you say?"

"I'll see you at seven," Sally answered. With that, the left his office, hoping he wouldn't change his mind.

Bryan tried to wrap his mind around what had just happened. Sally worked out front and dealt with all of the staff members, but only on work-related matters. Mr. Samuel's placed a lot of trust in her and her abilities. Recently, though, she had been making conversation with him and acting much friendlier. This could be an interesting evening.

After purchasing some beer and returning home from work, Bryan checked his e-mail. He had received a message: "Hello Bryan, this is Bill Majors from Majors and Jacobs Consulting. We took a close look at your résumé and were very impressed with your qualifications. On Monday, please give me a call, Frank Jacobs and I would like to discuss this with you. Kim or Kelly will answer the phone and they'll transfer you to me. I look forward to hearing from you."

Bryan clicked his mouse to the Write column and typed a reply: "Dear Mr. Majors, I received your e-mail and I will call you as you requested. Thanks for your reply. I look forward to talking to you. Bryan Wescott."

So now, Sally was having the time of her life in his bed and he was still sitting at his computer. He finished his beer and returned to the bedroom, where Sally was shaking on the bed, her eyes wide open as he switched the light back on. She seemed amazingly glad to see him. The vibrator and the tension on her breasts and nipples were achieving great success.

He sat beside her on the bed, thinking his sadism training from his college days seemed to be paying off. He massaged her pussy through the tape and wondered how much more she could take.

Her body stiffened and she arched her back. It was easy to see she was having another orgasm and in total release.

He gave her a few minutes to relax, then removed the tape and egg from her pussy. He took the weights and the clothespins off her nipples, but the string maintained its tight grip. He released her from her other bonds, removed the gag, and for the first time in three hours, she was free.

Sally sat up on the bed next to him and tried to relax, her hair falling across her breasts. "Bryan, that's one of the strongest orgasms I've ever had," she said. "When I was in college, I dated a guy and we made love three or four times a week. One night, he brought some rope into the bedroom and wanted to tie me to the bed. It sounded like fun, so I let him. From then on, almost every time we made love, I was tied to his bed, but it was never like what you just did to me. That's why I left so suddenly after the movie. It brought back too many memories from the past, and I wasn't sure I was ready for something like that to start again."

But she had returned, and Bryan knew she had made the commitment to follow her desires. It was easy to see she wanted to be his sex slave, but her training had barely begun. He wasn't even finished for the night yet.

"Walk to the end of the bed and face the headboard," he commanded.

"Yes, sir!" She surprised herself by how quickly and easily she answered him. This was another opportunity for her to explore her hidden desires. His words made her weak in the knees as she forced herself to stand up. She felt no shame at what they had just shared together, but it seemed selfish to want more. Maybe he was right; maybe she was a slut.

He watched her march to the end of the bed like a good little soldier, turn, and face forward, as he had requested. Bryan could tell by her expression that her fears and insecurities were very real, but her desire to face the unknown was too great.

He moved behind her and put the red ball gag to her lips. Without reservation, she opened her mouth and accepted the gag. He pulled her hair up, then, buckled the gag in place behind her head.

He attached black leather cuffs to each of her wrists and made her spread her legs. With short lengths of rope, he tied each ankle to the bed. "Lie forward on your stomach and put your hands and arms out in front of you," he directed.

Her heart pounded like that tribal drum she had heard earlier, and her mind raced at the thought that he might whip her again—or maybe put his cock in her; what an entertaining thought.

He attached a long piece of rope to each wrist cuff and tied the ropes to the headboard posts, spreading and pulling her arms as wide as her body would allow. This stretched her at the waist almost to the maximum. Her pussy slit and ass were now fully exposed and wide open to his view.

Bryan took a flogger out of his bag and began to stroke her ass, back, and pussy with light strokes. Stroke after stroke, the whip touched her body, and as the minutes passed, the severity of each stroke became more intense. Four. Five.

The sixth stroke was harder, and a squeal escaped from behind the gag. "*Eeha!*" Her body jerked to the sting of the whip, and red marks appeared on her skin from each of the leather thongs.

He stopped and started again slowly, then increased the severity. On the sixth stroke, another squeal echoed in the room. "*Eeha!*" She was losing control again. She struggled against the ropes holding her ankles and wrists; the bed shook, but the ropes held tight.

Bryan marveled at the incredible sight of her beautiful naked body positioned on the bed, compromised for the whip. He could feel the lust building in his loins as he watched her reactions to the stimulation. He dropped his shorts and started to stroke his already-hard cock. He was a little bigger than most, and very proud of his manly hood. The veins stood out and the smooth purple head showed he was ready to enter her.

He put his fingers in her pussy, and she moved her ass a little. Immediately, he knew she was dripping wet and ready. She relaxed to accommodate his penetration as he entered her, pumping in and almost out, slowly at first but then increasing the rhythm. She wiggled her ass a bit more and squeezed her inner muscles to hold his erection deep inside her.

He took his time, but when he was ready to send his cum to where it would do the most good, he held back. Her passion grew for her new Master because he waited until he thought she was ready. He felt her body tense and quiver at the same time. She exploded uncontrollably into an unbelievable orgasm, her body heaving out of control but going nowhere.

He let her finish and eased his cock from her vagina, then moved to sit at her front. He opened his legs and laid them across her outstretched arms, his still-hard cock wet with her cum and only inches from her head. Her face was down on the bed. He unbuckled the gag and eased it out of her mouth.

"Don't close your mouth," he whispered in the quiet room, her breath the only other sound that could be heard. He grabbed her hair and pulled her head up to face his raging cock. This was the first time she had actually seen his beautiful instrument of lust. He slid his manly hood deep into her open mouth, to the back of her throat. "Close your mouth and I *don't* want to feel any teeth! I like it like this!"

Her lips slowly closed around his cock, and with her tongue, she massaged the underside of his shaft. He used his grip on her hair to push and pull her lips along his hard rod. He threw his head back and pushed his cock forward until her nose touched his stomach. The feeling was astounding.

"*Ugh! Ugh!*" She heard the glorious sound of a man ready to come and felt his shaft grow stiffer in her mouth. His searing seed exploded against the back of her throat, almost making her gag. The smooth hot liquid slid down her throat, and her muscles took control as she sucked the remaining cum from his cock, something she had done before with the guy from college.

When he had finished, he pulled his cock slowly from her mouth. "Now *swallow* the rest of it!" She closed her mouth and swallowed the remaining liquid. He let her go and collapsed on the bed.

Several minutes passed before they could breathe normally, but they were young and recovered quickly. Bryan untied the ropes, cuffs, and string to free Sally. They sat on the bed together, and after a minute, she looked up at him with a submissive expression on her face that only a woman could understand. "I have never been so turned on in my entire life," she said. "Even with the guy I dated in college, it was never like this."

Bryan lightly kissed her lips and gazed deeply into her sparkling eyes. "It was great for me too. You are a beautiful and special woman, so vulnerable, and your willingness to surrender to a dominant shows so much character. It's very easy to see that anybody would be out of their mind if they didn't love you and your body—but I think it's time we took a shower!"

The Cabin (Chapter 2)

The shower helped soothe the aches in Sally's arm and leg muscles from the whip and those marvelous toys Bryan had used. She sat on his bed; drying her hair with the large beach towel he had given her, and watched him walk across the room toward her. Dressed in only a towel wrapped around his waist, he reminded her of a medieval warrior ready to take up his sword and do battle in some far-off land.

His words brought her back to reality: "Sally, do you remember when I told you about my golfing buddy who gave me the movie?"

"Yes, I remember," she answered. "He must be a very good friend to give you a movie like that."

"Yes, he is, a very good friend indeed," Bryan said. "He's got a cabin on this gorgeous lake about a four-hour drive north of here. He's been out of town for a few weeks and he asked me to check on the place. I need to drive up early in the morning, and I'd like you to go. I want to show you the house—I think you'll love it."

Sally was more interested in what had just happened to her than in a trip to the lake. "Where did you learn all those rope tricks and the other moves you put on me?"

"When I came to town for my job, I went on the Net and found a few people who enjoy the BDSM lifestyle as much as I do. I contacted them and made some friends. I'll tell you all about it in the morning. Will you go with me or not?"

"After what we did tonight, how can I say no?" Submitting to Bryan had quickly become a driving force for Sally. It wasn't just the sex act; she liked the way he took complete control of her. Something exciting was taking place in her mind and body, and she wasn't ready for it to end—not just yet, anyway.

"You'll have to spend the night," Bryan said.

She'd been waiting for him to mention it. "I expected to stay anyway," she said, maybe too quickly. He gave her a look that said her time, as his slave was not over.

"Your buddy's place must be really nice if he wants you to check on it," she continued.

"It is—you'll see. We'll have to leave early, so I think I'll make you a little more secure for the rest of the night. Are you ready to endure some more of my rope treatment?"

"I figured you'd do that," Sally said. Her body tingled with excitement at the thought of another round of helpless submission. She turned around on the bed and put her hands behind her back, just as an obedient little slave should do.

"Put your palms together." From the sound of his voice, she could tell he enjoyed giving her commands, and she enjoyed taking them. Sally wanted to tell him how intensely stimulating it was to be his submissive, but she was afraid that talking too much would take away from the experience.

Bryan looped a short rope around her wrists, pulled back with a reverse wind, and made a few loops between her wrists to secure the rope. After a double knot, her wrists were secure.

He wound a second rope around her elbows in the same way, and then pulled them together. As her arms were stretched behind her back, Sally looked down at her breasts and hard nipples jutting out in front. She was so proud of her body that she wanted to scream, "Please look at my body!"

After he tied her ankles together, all she could do was wiggle around on the bed. She could tell he enjoyed watching her struggle in the ropes.

"Oh! One last thing," he added, dangling the red ball gag in front of her face.

Sally's jaws still ached from the first time he'd used that thing. "No!" she said loudly, shaking her head. "Isn't tying me up enough?" She felt she had to make things a little difficult, or it would take all the fun out of it. She was careful, though—as sadistic as he was, she didn't want him going off any deep ends.

"Not tonight," he said. "I said, open your mouth!"

She realized he wasn't going to take no for an answer, so she humbly submitted and opened her mouth. The rigid gag slid back into place beyond her front teeth, and he buckled the leather strap behind her head. She could tell he'd used the next hole in the strap this time; the gag was much tighter than before.

"I'll untie you in the morning, my dear slave," he said with incredible politeness.

"Humm!" she moaned softly from behind the gag as the leather cut deeply into her cheeks. She wasn't sure she could handle that thing in her mouth all night. Of course, it really didn't make much difference; she knew she was going to have to deal with it, like it or not.

Bryan touched her warm, soft skin as he reached across her body to the nightstand and switched off the light. He patted her pussy a few times, letting her know that that was one of his most favorite parts of her body. "Good night, my little love slave. You have been such a pleasure for me tonight. Tomorrow, I'll see if I can make things a little more interesting."

As she lay in the silence of the cool, darkened room, Sally was lost in thoughts of the night's events. The security she felt in herself and the physical pleasure of submission was more than she had ever felt before. She wanted to continue, but she wasn't sure if this was the right choice for a new life. Bryan was a little more than she'd bargained for.

In the morning, he released her from the ropes, but before they left his apartment, he attached small adjustable metal clamps to each of her nipples. There was a thin silver chain attached to each clamp. The little beast's bit into her nipples, sending a sharp pain through her breasts, but after several minutes the pain eased. Trying to adjust to her new jewelry, Sally asked why he had used them.

"As my humble slave, I want you to always know your place and be ready to accept any cruelty I deem necessary. The nipple clamps will serve as a constant reminder," he told her.

They got into his car, and Bryan secured her to the bucket seat with the safety belt and handcuffed her hands behind the seat back. He only released her once during the trip, for breakfast and a rest stop. As they drove, the conversation turned to the cabin.

"Bryan, tell me more about the guy who owns this cabin," Sally said.

He gave her a warm, secretive smile, as if he knew something she didn't know and he wasn't going to tell her. "His name is Nick Baxter. He does architecture work for some high-class people, and he's been in New York for the last few weeks. We play golf from time to time, and he's become a very good friend. For the most part, he did the work on the cabin himself, but some friends helped. I've been out there several times, and it's quite a place." Sally could tell from Bryan's description that Nick might be a good person to get to know.

She didn't want to go into that with him right now, though, so she changed the subject. I've always been fascinated by being tied up and totally helpless. My only experience was with that guy from college, but I know we only scratched the surface."

"I want to know more about your love for tying up women and the BDSM lifestyle you referred to last night.

"You see, I'm a bit sadistic by some standards, and when I get a chance to be with a submissive, I like to keep her in restraints. That's why you're handcuffed now, and it just makes my cock so damn hard."

Bryan's mood changed a bit, and he said seriously, "you see, I enjoy young, attractive, and very submissive women who crave the activities we shared last night."

"Can I see it?" Sally asked before she realized what she had said. She licked her lips and wondered if he might show her his hard cock while he was driving. She wanted Bryan to know that she desired his cock and the submission she had

experienced the night before—that she wasn't just some stereotypical woman for him to take lightly.

"In due time. You'll just have to wait." He chuckled. "You know, I might be turning you into a little monster."

Sally was a little disappointed about not seeing his cock, but she didn't want him to wreck the car or something.

"See, many women have submissive feelings somewhere deep inside their souls," he continued. "I guess it's like living some sort of dark, mysterious fantasy." He glanced at her. "For me, I enjoy seeing my submissive's reactions to the kinds of things we did last night. I think it has something to do with being in control, having that incredible dominant power over a woman. You know, making you do things that you want to do, but in regular life you'd never do."

She relaxed a bit and tried to adjust her cuffed hands; the hard steel rings were digging deep into her tender wrists. He saw her struggle, and she could tell he enjoyed it. Maybe her movement was her way of getting back at Bryan for not showing her his cock.

"You seem to know a lot about women," Sally said, "and yes, it's an awesome feeling to be naked and restrained. I don't have to make any decisions or judgments—you have to do it for me. I'm actually forced to do your will."

"I don't know anything about that," he said. "I just watch and go with the flow, you know what I mean?"

It was late morning when they drove into a clearing overlooking the most beautiful lake that Sally had ever seen. Several large pine trees dotted the yard; the cabin wasn't just a cabin, but a beautiful log home. "This guy must have a lot of money to afford this!" she exclaimed. "Man, would you look at that lake?"

"He does really well." Bryan pulled into the driveway and stopped the car.

"I bet he does!" Sally decided Nick Baxter was definitely a man she might want to get to know.

They entered the house through the side door, and Bryan gave her a full tour of the place, ending with Nick's dungeon basement. The spacious room was dimly lit, but bright enough to see the complete area; when she realized what it was, Sally became even more excited. She'd thought he might take her to the master bedroom or something, but certainly not this.

In her childhood, Sally had read stories about beautiful women being taken prisoner and held for the lord of the castle. She remembered vivid dreams of soldiers stripping their captive and chaining her to a cold rock wall to wait for the dungeon master to arrive.

As Bryan took her arm to escort her around the room, she could see that it was full of everything you could ask for in a medieval dungeon. Several heavy, shiny chains of various lengths hung from pulleys in the ceiling, just waiting for a woman's wrists or ankles. A rack on the far wall held every kind of whip you could imagine, just hanging there, waiting to be used on someone's naked skin. There were other racks of implements as well, and all sorts of furniture designed for bondage and torture.

"Is this what I think it is?" She looked at the padded wooden horse and envisioned how her ass and pussy would be open, straddling it. Thinking about being tied to the frame intrigued her, but she didn't want to push the issue with Bryan; she wasn't quite ready to jump on the thing yet.

"That's right—it's a spanking horse. The submissive lies over it and puts her knees on the padded supports. Each leg has an eye-hook so her wrists and ankles can be tied or chained to the frame."

"I've seen this before in a couple of books, but never a real piece of furniture," Sally said. "I see how it could be very effective on a servant's backside." She could almost feel the rope tighten around her wrists and ankles, the burn on her ass from the whip, receiving whatever punishment he wanted to subject her to. It was a little hard to walk away, but there was so much else to see.

"What else is there?" Her excitement grew as he ushered her across the cool room to another torture device, and she smiled, knowing she was with her dungeon master.

"Over here." He pointed to a wood frame shaped like an X. "This is an X-frame, as you can tell by the wood configuration." He was like a teacher describing artwork in a museum. "Your submissive can stand facing forward or backward, depending on which part of the body you want to play with. Her wrists and ankles are secured against the frame."

Sally took several seconds to inspect the massive construction of the frame and its ability to restrain a person. Bryan chuckled, watching her walk around the wood structure. "Don't worry," he informed her, "once you're chained to the frame, you won't go anywhere. Everything is bolted to the floor with some very large bolts. I've got something else to show you. Come on."

He pointed to a large table looming in the darkness across the room. The menacing apparatus was a little frightening at first glance: laid out on the table were all sorts of leather cuffs, chains, and clamps, and attached to the front of the table was a very large ship's wheel with a long metal bar that held wrist chains.

"Okay, what's this?" Sally asked as they stopped beside the table. Her heart was racing to think he might use some or all of this equipment on her. The familiar feeling of total helplessness stirred in her stomach as she walked around the table inspecting the marvelous detail of the structure. She felt like someone in a furniture store looking at a kitchen table, but she knew better—this was a serious torture device.

"It's a stretching rack," Bryan explained. "The submissive lies on her back or her stomach and spreads her legs. Her ankles are cuffed and chained to the bottom legs of the rack, and her wrists are cuffed and chained above her head. That chain is controlled by the wheel." He turned the wheel a few times to demonstrate the tightness of the chains. "As the wheel turns, the body is stretched, and a tight body makes for a great reaction to a whip. Would you like to see how it feels, or look around some more?"

Bryan was having fun showing her the unique bondage equipment, Sally knew. She watched those sparkling eyes of his, and a small smirk appeared on her face. It was time for her to surrender to the submissive conscience that had invaded her soul. She ached to become that captive maiden, forced to endure some mysterious medieval ritual.

"I bet you'd like to see me on this rack, wouldn't you?" she asked him. Before he could answer, she turned around for him to unlock her handcuffs. He released her from the silvery cold steel; she quickly removed her clothes, and lay down on the rack. He immediately cuffed her ankles with the leather cuffs that were already attached to the ankle chains.

"Put your hands over your head." His masterful voice echoed in the room as it had done the night before. The dungeon master was ready to administer whatever punishment he desired. She hesitated for a few seconds, but then reminded herself that she yearned for the power exchange. As his slave of the chamber, she was ready to follow his satanic command.

The leather cuffs encircled both of her wrists, and he attached them to the wheel chain. She felt so gloriously wet and alive with anticipation of what was to come. The nipple clamps were still in place where he had put them that morning; she was experiencing no pain, but the clamps were an ever-present touch to keep her aroused for his pleasure.

Sally watched the way Bryan stood over her, ready to devour a naked woman in such a helpless position. She still had her eye on that beautiful erection under his shorts, and she hoped he would take them off soon. She wanted to feel his manhood in her mouth or any other opening in her body he wanted to use.

He turned the wheel a couple of times, and the chains tightened. She could feel the pull, but there was no pain—not yet, anyway. Sally knew what was coming next, but she wasn't prepared for the full intensity of pain that would forge through her sexually charged body.

Bryan took his time and watched her reaction as he turned the wheel a few more clicks. Her eyes closed, and a delicious feeling of helplessness rapidly invaded her body.

Lost in her dark world of submission, Sally forgot to look at Bryan's erection, now at its fullest. He stopped turning the wheel and stroked his cock a few times through his shorts; the temptation was too great for him to pass up.

She could hear the chain clank and another click of the wheel gear as it engaged again to the next notch. Her body felt the pull this time, and it left little doubt as to the purpose of the rack. "That's tight! Damn!" Sally gasped, trembling from the intense strain. She arched her back to try to reduce the pressure.

"That's not going to do any good, but you should know that from last night." Bryan's devilish smile signaled his haunting power over her; he knew she was about to embark on new territory. He turned the wheel again with no apparent warning, and it came to rest at the next gear slot.

"*Damn!*" she cried out, showing her pearly white teeth. She threw her head to one side, a grimace on her face, her eyes closed again.

He smiled at her and relished in the sight of her reaction. Her hair was a mess, and he tenderly gathered it up and smoothed it out.

Her arms and legs were stretched to their full extension, the strain quite evident, her ribs exposed and those beautiful breasts extended from her chest with the chained nipple clamps still attached. They were doing a fantastic job of keeping her nipples hard and sensitive. Bryan almost came from the sight of the painful rapture she was experiencing and the pulsing flame of vicious desire on her face. He knew she was at her limit, but he also could feel his power over her, and the possibility of taking her to new limits could not be denied. "Let's try one more click, what do you say? I'm sure you can take more."

Sally couldn't understand where he got that idea. She felt like her body was now at least 2 inches longer and still stretching. The pain increased; her ability to accept more was lost in her inner soul, but some deeper mystical strength required absolute submission.

"I don't—don't think I can handle any—*moorre*!" Her words and voice didn't seem to want to work. He engaged the wheel another click, she wanted to speak, scream something, but no sound would escape her mouth. At this point, she wasn't sure if she was doing this for his pleasure or for hers.

She had held tight to the conviction of her desire for torment, and now her reward was the pleasure she craved. He put his lips to hers and penetrated her mouth with his tongue. Her tongue darted against his, but it was out of control and she had no way of stopping it.

He ended the kiss, moved to the wall whip rack, and selected a riding crop with a wide flap-like end. She had seen and felt the same type of whip the night before, and she knew she could endure it; however, with her body stretched to its limit, it was a whole new ball game.

She watched him as he returned to her. He had taken off his shirt; now he was dressed in only his shorts and the whip in his hand to complete his ceremonial attire, standing over her like a medieval priest ready to perform some excruciating ritual.

He struck her right ass cheek twice. *Whap*! *Whap*! The sound cascaded through the room, leather on bare flesh. The dungeon master of the castle was taking her to new heights of torture and total submission. The pain was so intense that it was useless to struggle; she was a meager toy for his pleasure. She sensed Bryan had lost control of himself and all he wanted to do was to deliver punishing strokes to her bare flesh.

"*HeAHAA!*" she cried. Two small red marks that matched the end of the whip appeared on her skin. A third stroke hit just below the first two, making another red mark. "*HeAHAA!*" Sally shuddered as more strokes fell on her stomach and inner thighs, each leaving its mark.

He laid the wicked leather crop down on her stomach, separated her pussy lips with his fingers, and inserted his forefinger deep into her vagina. The entry gave her a devastatingly powerful, mystical feeling of pure sex. She wanted to wrap her legs around his finger and lose it inside her.

"Man, you're wet!" he said. "Even last night, you weren't this wet. You must love what I'm doing, don't you?"

Sally's chest was rising and falling from her labored breathing and the penetration of his finger. Her legs pulled on the ankle restraints, but her restricted movement left her still open and in the same position. The nipple clamps jutted into the air as she closed her eyes. "I love it, damn it, I *love* it! Don't stop!" she begged. "Please don't stop!"

Bryan's finger burned hot in her pussy for several minutes, but he had other things on his mind. The flame of desire did not leave Sally when he released the lock on the wheel, although the tension on her body eased. He unhooked her wrist and ankle cuffs from the rack, but left them attached to her. Slowly, she sat up on the edge of the table, her feet dangling just above the floor.

She cleared her throat. "That's an experience I'll never forget." The circulation was starting to return to her body, and she knew that as soon as it did she would explore another dark fantasy. She could hardly wait.

"Sally," he said, "you're an incredible woman. I know we stretched those limits of yours a little that time." He smiled at her like a little boy in a toy store. "Come on, I've got something else to show you."

Sally couldn't fathom what else he had in mind for her, but she followed him on shaky legs to the other side of the torture chamber.

"Look up," he said, pointing to the ceiling. She raised her head slowly to see a wire cable with an "O" ring attached to it, running over a pulley in the ceiling and attached to a winch that connected to a wooden wall support. She felt like the wicked "O" ring was laughing at her; it knew things she didn't know, but was about to find out.

Bryan cranked the handle on the winch, and the "O" ring dropped to her eye level. He took a large clip hook and attached it to her wrist cuffs and to the "O" ring. He reversed the crank on the winch, and her wrists and arms were lifted over her head, giving her the same sensation of stretching her body had felt on the rack. Her toes were now the only things touching the floor.

"How far are you going with this? My gosh! Bryan! How far are you going?"

Before she could finish her statement, he cranked the handle a few more times, and she put her head back. He stopped turning the winch when her toes were completely off the floor and she was suspended by her wrists. She hung there, her breath a little out of control, a helplessly bound slave woman stretched to the limit and waiting for her punishment.

"Okay up there?" he asked. She heard him talking, but couldn't answer. "You know, the marks from the rack are almost gone, and we can't have that, now can we? Let's see if I can put some more in their place—and I think it's time for a gag as well." He picked up a ball gag from the table next to the wall and showed it to her.

Sally had learned that swallowing before she took the gag in her mouth helped her accept it better. She closed her eyes and obediently opened her mouth; he inserted the gag and buckled the strap behind her head.

She took the ball further into her mouth this time, causing her lips to touch. She had hoped it would take off some of the pressure where the leather strap was cutting into her cheeks; instead, the leather dug too deeply, and she had to relax her mouth for the gag to return to its proper place. The pressure eased a little, but not much.

"My dear, I truly believe you were meant for bondage in every way. You are a beautiful woman, but bondage takes you to another level," Bryan said. "Now, let's see about some more marks."

He went back to the whip rack, and she watched him ponder another whip selection. She trembled a bit at the whip he chose; it looked more evil than any other whip she had seen.

"This small whip with the four poppers—it'll do just fine," he said, returning to her side.

She bit into the ball gag as he raised the whip in the air. The first stroke made contact with her left breast, snagging the nipple and the clamp. From somewhere behind the gag, she managed a scream. "*Ahee!*" she squealed in uncontrollable pain. Her body jerked out of control, and some drool oozed down her chin from the side of the gag. The second stroke was to her right breast, and produced the same effect. Red lines appeared on both breasts across her nipples.

Several more strokes produced more of the same. It was easy to see that Bryan was a master with the whip.

Now, he shifted his attention from whipping her breasts to her pussy. He had not secured her cuffed ankles in the suspension, and she was able to keep her legs together; he tried several times to whip her pussy, but was unable to reach the desired spot. Her upper thighs caught the stinging blows, and she knew her skin was ripping into shreds.

Finally, he laid the beastly thing down and picked up two long coils of three-quarter-inch rope. She watched as he tied the ropes to her ankle cuffs and secured them to opposite wall hooks across the room, spreading her legs and exposing every inch of her slit. She could feel her sex open, offering him an even better look.

Sweat formed on her chest and forehead; the exhilarating terror of more to come was at hand. Submissively, she suffered, knowing her pussy was in for an incredible experience.

He began slowly, lightly striking the folds of skin around her pussy with the whip. Her body responded with a small jerk, and a small flame of delight ignited inside her. It was in perfect harmony with what was to come—not that she wasn't already turned on, but her sexual desire was strengthening.

The whipping continued, causing her body to respond with more jerking and more sweat trickling down her cleavage. He loved to see her sweat. It was a game now. He would strike her pussy, stand back, and watch her body jerk.

He pulled her head back by her hair so that she couldn't see when the strike was coming; the surprise of the whip's sting and her wild contortions were a beautiful sight for him to watch. His strokes became harder and faster.

"*Ahee!*" She did a good job of getting noise around that gag. He hit her again.

"*Ahee!*" She pulled on the cable over her head and at the same time tried to pull her legs together, but her bonds held fast, not offering her an inch of grace. More drool oozed from behind the gag and ran down her chin.

He let go of her hair and stopped the whipping. She eased her head forward to see what he was doing. He touched her pussy and felt its heat, then inserted his finger as deeply into her vagina as he could go, causing her to gasp for air behind the gag.

"You're just as wet now as you were on the rack." The sound of his voice almost made her come—not that she hadn't already; she had lost count of how many times. All of the fiery pain she had just endured disappeared into a wondrous, haunting feeling of desire.

He removed his finger slowly, bent his head down, and put his tongue to her clit. His tongue took over the song his finger had just played. Several minutes passed, and he could tell from her body stiffening and her labored breathing that she was ready to come.

Her eyes were wide, pleading that he let her expel her cum for him. He stood up and gazed at her with those sparkling brown eyes, returning his finger to her pussy. "Are you ready to come for me?"

She wanted to tell him in so many ways that she had already come for him so many times, but alas, she was ready to do it one more time. *"Aha UMMM!"* she spit from behind the ball gag.

"Well, do it, then! *Do it now!"* he commanded.

She jerked her body again and tried to push her pussy against his finger as best she could. Her body stiffened, she held her breath, and the floodgates to her sex opened. That special feeling of release washed her away on an incredible orgasm.

Bryan quickly licked away the beads of sweat that ran down her chest and between her breasts. He took extra time on her nipples, sucking the rigid knobs and pulling them with his teeth. "I just love to taste your body sweat," he told her, licking his lips. "You taste so damn good, you know that?"

Some minutes later, he untied her ankles and let her down from her suspension. She sat on the floor for several minutes to get the blood circulating. When she was able to stand, he silently picked up his whip, put his arm around her waist, and escorted her to the spanking horse.

"Put your knees together on the side support of the bench. Bend at the waist and put your hands to the front and back legs of the bench on the other side."

It took her a minute or so to comply with his request, but he waited. Bent over as she was, her ass and pussy were wide open to his view. With small lengths of rope, he secured her cuffed wrists to the legs of the spanking horse.

"Spread your knees as wide as you can." His commands were short and to the point, and left nothing to be discussed. With each passing minute, Sally's life took a new turn as his sex slave. It made her feel strong and sensual to know she had this much power over a man. Although he was the master, she knew she was his and no other woman could touch him.

He secured her ankles on the other side of the spanking horse in the same fashion as her wrists, leaving her totally tied and spread. He was behind her, so she couldn't see him strip his shorts off and stroke his rock-hard cock. The familiar tingle in his balls signaled that he was about to come, but he didn't want to rush things, so he eased the strokes.

She felt him open her pussy as wide as it would go, and then the wonderful, fulfilling penetration of his cock sliding into her sex. "*Aha UMM!*" she moaned. She responded to his motion slowly at first, but soon he settled into a smooth in-and-out rhythm. She relaxed her legs and inner sex muscles as best she could to allow him full penetration. Her head was down and her hair almost touching the floor; he grabbed her waist with his left hand to steady his balance and pushed himself as deep into her as her body would allow.

He could feel the heat and wetness of her sex telling him that her body wanted more. With his right hand, he picked up the whip and gave her a swat across the ass. Her body stiffened and jerked from the stinging pain of the whip, and he knew she was ready to come again. Seconds later, her juices opened and she was swept away on another breathless orgasm.

When she finally relaxed after her orgasm, he released his grip on her waist and eased his cock out of her. Sally couldn't understand why he had taken the rapture of his cock away from her. Then, he walked around in front of her and pulled the gag from her mouth. Her jaws and cheeks ached, and being released from the gag was pure joy.

Bryan sat down on the floor in front of her, grabbed her hair again, and pulled her head up. Her eyes fixed on his hard cock, drowning in her own juices. "Keep your mouth open!" he ordered, and she knew what he had in mind.

He inserted his rigid cock fully into her mouth, the purple head touching the back of her throat. She closed her lips slowly around him and massaged the underside of his hard shaft with her tongue. Holding on to her hair, he pumped her head along the length of his cock with her mouth.

After a few seconds, he threw his head back and held his breath. *"Aha!*

Aha!" he grunted as his cum shot against her throat. "Keep it in your mouth, damn it, *keep it in your mouth!* Wait until you get it all!" He was gasping for air to get to his lungs. More cum oozed from the head of his hard cock.

His seed finally spent, Bryan eased his cock from her mouth. "Now, swallow it all."

When she didn't respond immediately, he picked up the whip and gave her ass cheek a hard blow, watching her writhe under the whip's sting. He could see her throat muscles pulsating as she swallowed his cum.

Several minutes passed before he released Sally from her restraints. She was now totally free for the first time in eight hours.

"Let's get a beer," he said. "I think both of us need one."

Bryan switched the lights off and locked the basement door as they went upstairs.

The New Toy (Chapter 3)

They left for home early the next morning, with Sally secured to the car seat by the safety belt and handcuffed just as she had been the previous day. Many things had happened to Sally in the last two days. Her spirit was alive for the first time since her college days, and Bryan was to thank for it. She loved the cabin, and the medieval torture basement was in a class by itself.

Her thoughts took her back to the night before and the vast amount of bondage furniture that Nick possessed. Bryan had tested her limits far beyond what she felt she knew them to be.

"Bryan, about Nick's bondage equipment," she asked, "where did he get all that stuff?"

"Well," he replied, "some people collect stamps, and Nick, he collects bondage equipment. Some of it he buys, and other things he makes himself. He's quite good at it."

"I'd like to meet him sometime. He sounds like a great guy." Bryan nodded. "I'll see what I can do. He should be back in a few weeks, and maybe we can visit again. I'm sure you'd like to make another trip to his basement— there are some things you didn't see, and I'd like to see if you can handle them."

Bryan released her from the cuffs and the seatbelt when they arrived back at his apartment. "I know we did a lot of unusual things this weekend," he said. "Are you okay?" There was concern in his voice. He hadn't expected to do so much, but one thing just led to another.

"A little sore, but I'm okay." Her voice turned serious and sincere. "Bryan, this weekend is one I'll never forget. As a little girl, I went to bed at night and fantasized about things like that—things that men would do to women. You know that guy I told you about from college. We did some fun things, but nothing like what you did to me. I can't imagine what else you could do to me. Thank you for taking me to a place I've always wanted to go but could never get to."

"Sally, you are a very special woman," he said. "I've been with a lot of submissive women since I moved here, and you are by far the most exciting person I've met."

She felt the softness in his lips as he lightly kissed her. She returned the sensuous kiss, then waved and got into her car.

As Bryan watched her drive off, he thought to himself, *She's still got those nipple clamps on.*

On Monday, the firm was unusually busy with all kinds of incoming calls and visitors. Only at lunch did Bryan step out to make his phone call to Bill Majors concerning his resume. Two rings and the voice of an angel from the heavens answered: "This is Majors and Jacobs, Financial Consultants, I'm Kim, and how may I direct your call?"

Sometimes the sound of a woman's voice can strike a man in both heads.

Kim's voice had a soft sound with definite signs of mystery and submission, and at the same time, an undeniable strength. Bryan struggled with the thought, if she looked as good as she sounded; he was truly a blessed man.

Returning to reality, he said, "This is Bryan Wescott calling for Mr. Bill Majors. He asked me to call today."

"Oh, yes!" the angel named Kim replied. "Mr. Majors said you might be calling. Please hold while I transfer you." There was a soft sound of beach music in the background, but Bryan couldn't forget the incredible voice he had just heard.

"*Bryan!*" Bill Majors answered in a pleasant but hearty voice. "I was anticipating you'd call. Frank Jacobs and I have reviewed your resume, and we're very impressed with what came up. We took the liberty and checked your references, even your college background. You have some very good people who think a lot of you and your abilities."

"Thank you, sir!" Bryan was astonished at what Bill had said. His confidence level inched up a bit.

"Bryan, let me tell you a little bit about us," Bill continued. "Frank and I started this company about five years ago, and it's been very successful. We now have eleven consultants, plus an office staff to handle our business. Generally, we help potential investors select companies to invest in; they make money, and that's how we make ours. In the last several months, we've been very surprised with overseas connections, and we feel we need another consultant to help in this area. If you're interested in talking about this further, I'd like to set up an interview with you this Saturday?

Bryan couldn't believe what he had just heard. *Things just don't happen like this—or do they?* He looked up from the phone booth, his stomach a mass of knots. Then he returned to the telephone.

"Sir, you do know that I'm in the Denver area?"

"There's no problem with that," Bill responded. "I'll fly you out on Friday evening and we can meet Saturday morning around ten. Kim will pick you up at the airport and get you settled for the night. We've got a nice place here for you to stay."

"How can I say no? I'll see you then."

"Okay, great! Hold on—I'll get Kim back on the line and she'll set things up."

A minute or so went by with more beach music in the background; then the angel returned to the telephone. "Mr. Wescott, are you there?"

"Oh, yes! Yes, I'm still here," Bryan said, anxious and a little unsteady.

"Great! I've got you booked out of Denver at 3:00 PM and arriving here about 10:30 PM our time. There will be an e-ticket for you at the terminal, and I'll meet you when you land."

"Yes, that's fine with me. I'm looking forward to seeing you." Bryan hung up the telephone and returned to work, shocked but pleased at what had just taken place. This was by far the most promising job offer he had ever had. He would really have to be on his toes for this interview.

Later in the day, Sally stopped by Bryan's office and put a ledger and a small envelope on his desk. "Sara gave this to me. It's the ledger with the records for the last quarter of this year. I can come by Wednesday evening and get it back, if that's okay with you? We'll need it this weekend for a meeting to go over the last details for our purchase, I hope?" She seemed a little unsure that the deal would go through

"Good, Wednesday will be just fine," he told her. "That'll give me plenty of time to take a good look at it, and I've got some other things I need to discuss with you. Who knows, we might even get a chance for a little spanking session—what do you think?"

"Bryan! Keep your voice down. Somebody might hear."

"Okay, okay," he replied with a chuckle in his voice. Sally left the office as Bryan opened the small envelope. To his surprise, it held the two nipple clamps from the past weekend. *She should have known better; I thought she would still be wearing them.*

On Wednesday night, Sally appeared at Bryan's door as promised. They sat down on the couch, and he wanted to tell her about his upcoming trip, but the ledger came first.

"Please tell Sara that I'm very impressed—I think she did an outstanding professional job," he said.

"She'll be pleased to hear that. So you don't think we'll be making a mistake?"

"Of course no one can predict the future, but I think you'll have a better than even chance to make it work."

"Would you like to go see the place with us Saturday?" Sally asked. "We'll only be there a short while."

"Thanks for asking, but I need to tell you something. I have an interview on the East Coast with a consultant firm. They're flying me out on Friday and I'm taking a half day off to make the trip. I'll be back Sunday night."

Sally was stunned by the news that Bryan might be taking another job. She had hoped her relationship with him would continue. Still, she was going to be leaving soon if her deal went through, and that would make things even more difficult.

She nodded. "I guess it'll be some time before we have a chance to see each other again?"

Bryan put his arm around her and pulled her to his chest. It was quite evident from the heat of her body that she was aroused. He gave her a long and romantic kiss; their tongues danced to that special tune they had experienced the past weekend. After a few minutes of this, Bryan whispered, "It's time to get those clothes off."

In seconds Sally stood before him in all of her naked splendor. Her skin was slick and smooth, a vision of loveliness. Her lack of pubic hair and fabulous naked breasts invited a touch from anything. Her legs were slightly parted; her slit open just enough to make his cock intensely hard.

"Put your knees on the couch and face the back, with your hands over the back of the couch. I want to see that pretty ass of yours," he ordered.

"You do have a way with words, don't you?" Again, she followed his instructions without hesitation.

He tied her wrists together with soft cotton rope and secured them to the back legs of the couch. Her knees pressed into the seat of the couch, and her head hung over its back. With a second long piece of rope, he tied both her ankles to the front legs of the couch. Her ass was forced up and wide open for the spanking that he had promised.

"Don't want the neighbors to hear any loud noises, you know." He showed her the all-too-familiar ball gag. "Okay, open that pretty mouth of yours." She took the gag beyond her front teeth as she had been trained to do, and Bryan completed the gagging by buckling the strap behind her head. Sally felt that mysterious helpless feeling wash over her body, powerless to stop Bryan from doing anything he wanted to do to her. She only wished she could make Bryan understand the excitement she felt. Her mind raced each time he touched her, with his hand or with the whip. Some might think it was humiliating, but it fulfilled her deep desire for submission.

He studied her round ass for a few seconds and lightly rubbed both cheeks with his hand. It was a delightfully sensual feeling. She wiggled he ass, telling him she wanted more. He loved to watch her respond to his touch.

"I think I'll use the small whip this time," he said. "I know you like that one." He had put it on the coffee table before she arrived with the anticipation of using it. The handle was about eight inches long, with two eight-inch leather leads at the end. He held it in front of her face and watched her eyes widen, knowing what was to come. "It's got a lot of sting to it, as you well know. When I finish, you'll have to tell me."

He began to strike her ass in a criss-cross fashion, not too hard at first, but enough to make the sound of leather on bare female flesh echo in the room. She moved her head and ass each time the whip made contact, but said nothing. *Bryan was right,* she thought, *there is a lot of sting.*

He moved the whip from her ass to her shoulders, her back, and then back down to her ass, watching her skin turn pink and red under his strokes. He stopped, walked around the back of the couch, and kissed her lips just to the side of the gag, then lightly bit her neck.

"*Mmmmm,*" she moaned from behind the gag.

"Feel good? It's always nice to have a little pleasure with your pain, don't you think?" Hearing his soft and sensual voice and smelling his body, she'd almost lost control and had her first orgasm. There was no restraint on her head except for the gag, so she nodded yes.

"Do you want me to continue? I can stop if you like." He knew she wanted more, but asking made the decision hers.

Again, she nodded.   She was where she wanted to be, blissfully under his control.   He started the whipping again, and this time the strokes were much harder and faster. The echo of his whip hitting her flesh rebounded off the room walls with a devilish sound. He was beginning to understand her incredible desire for submission.

"*Ahee! Ahee!* Sounds of pain escaped the ball gag. The skin around her ass became increasingly red with each stroke. Red lines marked her back, shoulders, and ass. Each stroke brought another muffled scream of pain. Some drool began to ooze from the side of the gag in Sally's mouth and trickle down her chin.

Bryan dropped the whip and his shorts almost in the same instance. His cock, rock-hard, jumped out of his shorts, the purple head bounced with anticipation. This beautiful lady with the most gorgeous pussy you ever laid your eyes on was waiting for his penetration.

He opened her pussy lips with his left hand, and a second later slid his massive cock into her sex canal until it disappeared. He started his pumping motion, slow at first, in and out, increasing as time went on. He was not in any hurry. She tried to move her ass to his cadence, but could only move a little, considering her position.

It wasn't long before the tingle started in his balls, but he held back; he could tell she wasn't ready to come. He had been with her long enough to know when her body was ready to give in to her lust, and she was not there yet.

On and on, he continued his slow pumping action, yet she would not fully respond. He reached for the whip he had laid beside her and struck her back, shoulders, and the top of her ass, solidly and even harder than before. She threw her head back, her hair flying in all directions, and yelled through the gag, "*Edddie!*" Her body stiffened, and she pushed her pussy and ass as far back as the ropes would allow, yearning for the full feeling of Bryan's cock deep inside her inner core. She came and came as hard as she could. Bryan gritted his teeth, and his body stiffened at the feel of her lust; then he filled her pussy with a massive load of his cum. Sweat poured from their skin, glistening in the light of the room. The smell of sex cascaded in the air as he lay across her back, totally spent.

He removed all of Sally's restraints, including the gag. They slid down the couch and held each other for a very long time, her head resting on his shoulder.

"Bryan," Sally whispered. "The guy I told you about from college—it was just a little tying up, maybe spread-eagle a bit, but it was never like this. I needed more and more to get off. All he did was tie me tighter and in different positions. I've been afraid to let myself go and enjoy my body, but you seem to know what to do."

"I understand. This past weekend and now tonight. I guess I'll just have to continue to be innovative, won't I?"

"I certainly hope so."

"I've got something for you," he said.

"Oh!" She looked up like an excited child at Christmas. "Well, what have you gone and done for me?" They both sat up, and Bryan pulled a small bag from under the couch and gave it to her.

"Sorry I didn't wrap it, but at least you know I was thinking 'bout ya." He smiled as she opened the bag and took out a box labeled "Dog Collar."

"Damn, Bryan, I know you're training me to be your sex slave, but this—are you trying to make me into a puppy or something?" She gave him a puzzled look, and then opened the box to reveal a small leather belt.

"Put it around your waist and buckle it," he told her. "Make it tight but not uncomfortable."

As she did so, she noticed a small control box on the belt next to the buckle, with a little wire that was hanging loose. There was a small "D" ring attached to the buckle of the belt. On the back of the belt was a leather loop.

"Okay," she said, "what happens next?"

Bryan reached into the box and pulled out a white metallic-web strap. At each end were small plastic clips. "Stand up and turn around." He snapped one clip to the belt loop at the crack of her ass. "Turn around, face me, and spread your legs." He reached between her legs, grabbed the webbed strap, and pulled it through the crack of her ass, tight enough for it to disappear into her pussy. He snapped the other plastic clip to the "D" ring at the buckle, then attached the small loose wire of the control box to the webbing.

"I'm a little confused," she said, looking at the belt. "It's a very unusual G-string."

"Walk to the other side of the room."

She took five steps across the room, then stopped, turned around, and stared at him. While she moved across the room, Bryan reached into the package and pulled out a control box, about the size of a car lock control. It had four buttons: "Power," "L," "M," and "H." He pushed the Power button and a small LED came on. Then he held down the "L" button for a few seconds.

Sally suddenly started looking around for the electric eel that had invaded her sex.

"*Aheee! Aheee!*" she screamed. Her hands went to her sides, and she almost lost her balance as her knees buckled. The sudden electric shock between her legs was like being lost in a wasteland with no way out.

She tried to catch her breath. It was a feeling she had never experienced before. It was a double-edged sword, the thrill of something pulled tight in her pussy, but the electrifying pain was frightening.

He gave her a few seconds, and then pushed the same button again. She opened her mouth, but nothing came out. Her eyes widened and her knees buckled again. She closed her legs and shook her head, her hair flying in all directions. She tried to do something with her hands, but didn't know what to do with them. Bryan held the button for a few seconds and watched the show as she jerked around completely out of control.

"The shock goes through my whole body, Bryan. I— I don't think I can stand much of this." Her voice was desperate.

He made her walk to different parts of the room and to other rooms of the apartment. From time to time, he would push one of the buttons. For the next thirty minutes, he watched an incredible dance, a show of magical proportions.

"How wet are you?" he asked finally, knowing she was experiencing a beautiful landscape from another planet.

"How wet is a river?" she replied. Bryan could see oceans of sweat glistening on her cleavage and upper thighs.

"I hope you like your new toy?" He'd known all along that she would love it. Exploiting another form of submission was certainly challenging.

"It'll take a little getting used to, but I'll try," she said. "This is really sweet, but I've got to get up early. Will I see you tomorrow?"

"No, I'm afraid not—I have to visit those last four new clients, but I'll be in Friday morning. Make sure you wear your new toy." She dressed with the belt still on, picked up the ledger, and left his apartment. As she walked to her car, Bryan watched from his window. She looked up, and he pressed the "H" button.

She hadn't expected anything else. The shock was strong, but she could handle it. She opened the car door, shook her pretty head, and found the strength to wave goodbye.

He turned the controller off; he didn't want to use up the batteries.

Friday morning, Bryan arrived early to prepare for his trip. After things settled down, he looked out of his office door and saw Sally moving papers around on her desk. No one was anywhere in sight, so he pulled the small control box out of his pocket. The LED blinked on, and he pushed the "L" button.

Sally dropped her papers and almost fell out of her chair. He saw the same amazing, desperate look on her face that he had seen on Wednesday night. It was priceless.

A few moments later, his office telephone rang.

"And a good morning to you too!" Sally said on the other end. He could hear her trying to catch her breath.

"Did I catch you at a bad time, my dear?" Bryan said, chuckling.

"I'll just have to do better, that's all." Her control was starting to return.

"I'm sure you will. It just takes a little getting used to, remember?" he informed her.

It was almost lunchtime when he finally finished his last set of papers. He eased from his chair, walked to the office door, and looked toward Sally's desk, hoping she would be alone.

Mary, one of the other staff members, was there talking to her. He waited until she left, then touched the "L" button on the control box. Sally jerked her head back and dropped an armful of papers, but immediately picked them up and continued with her work. Bryan chuckled; he could see the stress in her face, but she was getting better at the game.

Nothing else happened until lunch, when most of the staff left the office. Bryan packed his things, turned off his office light, and walked by Sally's desk; she was just getting ready for lunch herself.

"I should be back late Sunday; I'll give you a call," he said.

She looked at him, a little unsure of what he might do. "Sara and I should be back

about the same time. If you get back first, just leave me a message on the box and I'll call you back. Have a safe trip."

"You too," he said, "and I hope the rest of the day will be a little less electrifying than the morning has been." He loved to tease her that way.

"Thanks." She winked.

With that, he left for the airport.

The Interview (Chapter 4)

The plane banked to the right for its final approach for landing as Bryan's thoughts raced back to the telephone conversation with Kim and her voice from heaven. If her features were anything like she sounded on the phone, she would be an angel indeed.

There were only a few people in the lobby; he easily spotted her, holding a card with his name on it.

"Hi! I'm Bryan Wescott, and you must be Kim?" He smiled softly and pleasingly as he spoke, admiring her amazing eyes and smile. A woman's eyes told volumes about her, and Kim's were incredible. Her body radiated energy and composure. Even compared to his lovely sex slave Sally, Kim took center stage. Bryan could just look at a woman and know she tasted good; Kim was a king's feast just waiting for a picnic table.

"Yep, that's me." Her tone was friendly and confident, but yes, Bryan detected a hint of submission. He was always on the lookout for that. "I'm Kim Hazlewood," she continued. "How was your flight, and do you have any luggage?"

"Ah yes," he replied, returning to reality. "The flight was great, and yes, I've got one bag." He held out his hand, and she took it and held it for a few seconds. Bryan could feel the warmth and softness in her touch. He also felt strength in her hand that suggested she was athletic.

"Okay, great," she responded. "I know where the baggage claims are, so just follow me."

As they left the plush lobby, Bryan surveyed the contours of Kim's body. Just the

thought of her naked and handcuffed to the bedposts sent a thrill through his loins. They retrieved his bag, and within minutes, were leaving the parking lot.

"Just sit back and enjoy the ride," she told him as he watched the airport disappear from sight. After such a long flight, the drive along the coast highway was pleasant and relaxing.

"Some view," she said, trying to break the ice.

"You bet," he replied. The city lights in the distance reminded him of the stars in the western sky at night; you could almost reach out and touch them. It was electrifying sitting beside her in the car. He could sense her body heat.

"Just wait until you see where you'll stay tonight," she said. "I think you'll be pleased."

He could tell she wanted the trip to go well. She kept looking at him surreptitiously, and he hoped she was as pleased with her new acquaintance as he was.

Bryan could see several lights ahead as Kim slowed to pull into a driveway. The American flag and state flag waved in the light ocean breeze outside the building. To the left of the red brick entrance, a large green sign trimmed in gold read, "Windsor Shades Country Club and Estates."

"Do we have a tee time or something?" Bryan asked jokingly, a little surprised at the sign.

"No! Not tonight." Kim laughed and put her hand to her mouth. "We have several homes and townhouses around the golf course, and you'll be staying in one for the next two nights."

She stopped the car at the security station, and a guard stepped out from behind a windowed door. He bent down and looked into the car.

"Hi, Ray!" Kim said. "This is Bryan Wescott. He'll be spending a couple of days with us."

"Yep, got it right here," Ray said, looking at his logbook. "Welcome, Mr. Wescott, I hope you enjoy your stay. Kim, Mr. Majors said to give you 21. Sam's got the keys at the office." He was polite, but very professional. Bryan liked that in a person.

"Gosh, what a beautiful building," he said as they drove on.

"That's the main clubhouse," Kim said. "It took about two years to complete the construction."

"I must say, it's nice." Bryan continued to stare at the clubhouse. It reminded him of a Southern plantation house, with the large white majestic columns adorning the front.

They drove around the building and into a very large parking lot dotted with parked cars. As they drove to the far end of the lot, he noticed a small paved road that led to an older building surrounded by a stone wall. There were only a few lights around the front door; it was a very dark, desolate-looking place. He was going to ask Kim about the old building but she answered before he could ask the question.

"They call it the Club. It's actually the old golf clubhouse," she said. "They use it for private events and local group socials, or at least that's what they call them. Some of the club's executives have offices upstairs."

She pulled the car to a stop in front of a small administration building. They walked in and Kim rang the bell on the counter. An elderly man came in from the next room.

"Hi, Sam!" Kim said with a snap in her voice. "This is Bryan Wescott. He has a meeting with Bill tomorrow, and Ray said you have the keys to 21?"

Sam took down a set of keys from the wall and gave them to her.

"He knows everyone that stays here," Kim said to Bryan, "and he'll talk you to death if you let him."

"Watch her, son." Sam smiled and touched her hand. "She's a mess."

"Don't worry, sir, I've got my eye on her." Bryan could tell that Sam liked Kim, in a fatherly way. There was a lot of respect there. He wondered if Sam knew what he was really thinking.

Kim turned her head a little in his direction. "Is that right?" she asked, smiling. "I better watch out for you."

They left the office and Kim showed Bryan to his condo. He was pleased with it. "Thanks, Kim, this is just great."

"Okay, I'll get you at eight," she said. "Your meeting is at ten, but it'll give us a chance to get some breakfast. I need to check on Kelly and Peggy at the Club. We tend bar there from time to time, especially when they have events. I'll see you in the morning."

After breakfast, they drove into the city. Just before the turn-off to the office, they passed a place called the Castaway Club, and the advertisement on the front of the building made Bryan sit up and take notice. Prominently displayed on the sign were two seductive, scantily clad women wearing handcuffs and chains. The sight of women in bondage and the possibilities that might be afoot attracted Bryan like a magnet draws iron.

"Is that a strip club or something?" he asked, knowing the answer before he asked the question. He tried to appear inquisitive; he didn't want to rock any boats yet.

"You might want to stay out of that place," Kim said, observing Bryan's interest. "They get a little wild in there sometimes."

"It just looks like a strip joint. Am I missing something here?"

"You pay a cover charge when you go in, and then a hostess presses a button and lets you through an inside door. They do all kinds of bondage play and just about anything else."

"Sounds like you've been there," he said. This was a conversation he wanted to pursue.

"Kelly, Peggy, and I have been in a few times to check the place out. People go there because they want to, and they seem to enjoy themselves. I guess you could say it's a personal private place. It's a place without anyone nagging you where you can take full pleasure in all your senses and emotions."

"This place sounds like it has everything that anyone interested in BDSM could ask for," Bryan said, pushing Kim's envelope. "What else can you tell me about it?"

"I shouldn't be talking about this with you," she said. "I hardly know you."

"It's okay. I have some friends out West who are involved in a few things like this."

"Well, okay, but you can't say anything, promise?"

"Don't worry, Kim," he assured her, "I don't talk out of school."

"Well, the last time I went in, Kelly and Peggy just trotted off and left me sitting in the corner. I saw this Mistress working with a very attractive submissive woman, and boy, was she mad. She had her hands cuffed and pulled over her head, and her feet were just barely touching the floor. She called the submissive a slut and said she was going to teach her a few hard lessons about leaving that bastard boyfriend of hers.

"The flogger made her back so red and sensitive—I could tell by the way her body jerked after each stroke. I could hardly control myself, it was so exciting. The girl whimpered every time she got hit, and the Mistress was so upset that she put a gag in her mouth.

"After a whipping that seemed to go on forever, she made the girl get down on her stomach and put a piece of heavy paper on her back. From her toy bag, she pulled out a knife and traced the lines on the paper, cutting lines into the girl's back. When the Mistress pulled the paper away, a picture of a rose was etched into her skin. I could see droplets of blood oozing from the scratches.

"She cleaned her off with a towel and watched the scratches bleed until she was sure there was enough blood, then took a piece of canvas, lay it over the scratches, and pressed it down. A picture of a rose in blood appeared on the canvas. She set it aside on another towel to dry."

"Sounds like that Mistress was leaving her personal mark on her back," Bryan said. He had listened with extreme interest. Maybe she was going too far, but he cherished everything she was saying. He could tell she was well versed in BDSM play, but he didn't want to push her; he wanted her to take the lead.

Kim continued her story. He thought she was enjoying it.

"The Mistress stood the girl up and prominently displayed the rose on her back to the audience. She advised the sub that it would happen again if she forgot her place, and that she was going to frame the cloth and give it to her as a reminder. When she took the gag out of the girl's mouth, she could hardly speak, but finally said she understood."

"That's quite a story," Bryan said. He had almost gotten a hard-on listening to her, but he was trying to compose himself. He had to remember that he was there for a job interview, not an encounter with a submissive.

"Don't you dare tell anyone I told you about this," Kim said. "I could lose my job."

"Your story is safe with me, it's okay." Bryan was warming to this incredible woman. It was going to be interesting to find out how submissive she was. A practiced sadist is always looking for his next encounter.

"Here we are," she informed him.

They entered the elaborate twelve-story high-rise, took the elevator to the fourth floor, and stepped through the glass double door engraved with "Majors and Jacobs Consulting Firm." Just inside the door was a large reception desk, and Bryan did a double-take when he saw the two gorgeous women who were standing there talking. He couldn't believe there were so many beautiful women here.

"Kelly Wagner, Peggy Brown, this is Bryan Wescott." Kim introduced Bryan to her co-workers. The greeting was sociable, but he could tell there was more to these women, especially with Kelly. She stood out as a woman at the top of her field, but what field was that? Bryan couldn't put his finger on it, but there was certainly more to her than just being a receptionist.

"Mr. Majors just called," Kelly said, shrewdly glancing at Bryan.

"Bryan—is it okay if I call you Bryan? He's running a minute or two late, but he should be here soon."

"Yes, by all means." He was feeling a little apprehensive, but still in control.

"Would you like some coffee while you wait?" she asked him.

"Black with two sugars would be fine."

"I'll get it," Peggy offered, and left the desk area. She soon returned with Bryan's coffee.

A few minutes later, a tall, strong, athletic-looking man entered the lobby where Bryan was sitting. He watched as Kim stood up to greet the man. "Here's Mr. Majors now. Mr. Bill Majors, this is Mr. Bryan Wescott."

Bryan stood up, and they shook hands.

"Sorry I'm a bit late," Bill said. "Things happen, you know. Come on back to the office and bring your coffee." He gestured for Bryan to follow. "Kim, we'll be about an hour. I just saw Frank come in the other door; please give him a call and let him know we're ready."

"Sure thing. I have to run to town, but I'll be back by the time you finish."

Bryan followed Bill down the hall and into his large office. They sat down in lounge chairs at the coffee table in front of his desk. Frank Jacobs came into the office a moment later, and they shook hands as Bill introduced Frank to Bryan.

"I hope you had a nice flight and your accommodations are adequate?" Bill asked. "Absolutely. I'm very comfortable, thank you."

Frank sat back in his chair and eyed Bryan. "Let me tell you a little about what we do here," Frank said. "Bill and I were CPAs, and over the years, we became very good friends. We both had clients with large sums of money who had asked us how to invest safely, so Bill and I talked about it, and eventually, we started this firm. Now, five years later, we have a staff of eleven consultants, two accountants, and three receptionists. In the last six months, we've received several calls from potential international clients who want to invest in US companies. We're looking for a reliable new employee to deal with these types of investors."

"Bryan," Bill interrupted, "how do you feel about working with clients at the international level?"

"I've never worked with out-of-country investors before," Bryan said, some concern in his voice, "but I'm sure it will be very challenging. I'm willing to give it a try."

"Another thing," Bill continued. "What we look for in new employees are young, aggressive people. We train them in how we do business, but we want to tap their abilities to make money. That's what we do; we make money for others, and in turn it makes money for us."

"If we select you, Bryan," Frank added, "we'll start you at $50,000 a year, and after a six-month probation time, we'll think about an increase.

We'll also put you on a commission program over and above your regular salary, and provide all the other benefits. Do you have any questions for either of us at this time?"

No, sir, not right now, but I'm sure I'll have some." Bryan was feeling better about the interview. It just felt right.

"As I told you on the phone," Bill said, "Frank and I took the liberty of checking your references. We want the right person in the right job; that's why we had you fly in. We feel you can help this firm and yourself advance in the business world."

"I have wanted to work in the consultant area for a long time," Bryan said. "As you know, living in a small town and doing what I'm doing now, I could be there for the next 25 years doing the same job. I want to move ahead."

"Frank and I will review all the information we have, and by next Wednesday we'll call and let you know our decision," Bill said. "Kim should be back by now, and I've asked her to show you around the city and some of its most interesting places. I want you to join us for dinner tonight. The Club Restaurant puts on a real good evening meal, and I think you'll like it. Virginia, Frank, and his wife will join us. I've asked Kim to be your escort, if that's okay?"

"Wonderful. I look forward to it."

Kim stuck her head in the door. "I'm back. Are you guys finished?"

"Yep, Kim, he's all yours," said Bill. "Dinner's at seven."

"Not a problem, we'll be there. Well, Mr. Wescott, are you ready for the nickel tour?"

"You bet." He couldn't think of anything else to say.

The men shook hands, and Bryan left with Kim.

"Well, what do you think?" Bill asked.

Frank sat up in his chair. "You know, he might be our guy. I think he has a lot of promise. He reminds me of us when we first started. He wants to get out of that small- town rut and do some interesting things."

"I agree," said Bill. "What about our other two interviews?"

Frank hesitated for a few seconds. "Our lady June, she's expecting a baby in a few months. She's very smart and talented, but I don't think she could put the time and effort into what we need at this time."

"What about our guy Jack?" Bill asked. "You know, he did very well in the interview."

"Jack is very young," Frank said. "He has the talent, his grades are great, and I think he might be of help to us, but not now. He needs more experience."

"Well then, Frank, I think we've already made up our minds and hired Bryan. I do want to see how he acts around other people first—that's why I wanted him to have dinner with us."

"I understand," Frank replied. "I think that's a great idea."

"Did you have Kelly's people in Washington check him out? And what about your people?"

"Oh, yes!" Bill was quick to answer. "Kelly's people didn't find anything on the books about any of the three we've talked to. My people, the same thing."

"Okay, then," Frank said, standing up to leave. "Let's see how tonight goes, but I'm sure it will go fine. We can get together on Monday and make a final decision."

The Castaway Club (Chapter 5)

On their return through town, Kim drove past the Castaway Club again. Bryan wasn't sure if she went by the place on purpose or by accident, but he noticed that the parking lot was almost full of cars. The idea that a woman as beautiful and sexy as Kim might enjoy the place was appealing to him.

"They must do a lot of business in there," he commented, hoping she would get the idea and stop.

"I guess you want to see what it's all about, don't you?" Kim replied.

"I must admit, I do."

"Okay," she said after a moment, not sure if this was the right thing to do. She turned the car into the lot. "You know," she said, turning to face Bryan, "I'm not supposed to take you here; this isn't part of the tour. If I take you in, you've got to promise me you won't say anything to anyone about what you see or hear."

"Don't worry, Kim, I understand," Bryan said. He could tell that she was a little anxious, but he sensed she wanted to go in herself.

When they entered the club, they were greeted by another attractive young woman behind a small counter by the door. It seemed like no matter where Bryan went; there was one beautiful young woman after another.

She had short black hair and was wearing a black leather halter top that hardly covered her nipples, exposing a cosmic pair of breasts.

A small padlock, the type you would use on a suitcase, secured a black leather collar around her seductive neck, and she wore a similar leather cuff on each of her wrists. He couldn't see below her waist, but could only imagine she had very little on.

"Hi, Carol. This is Bryan Wescott—he's in town for a couple of days," Kim said to her. "He had an interview with Bill this morning about a new job."

"That's great." Carol smiled, giving Bryan the once-over. "Kim, he's a nice hunk. Nice to meet you, Bryan." She put her hand out, and they shook hands.

"Nice to meet you too." Bryan enjoyed her soft, exotic touch, not to mention her compliment.

Carol's eyes never left Bryan's face as she asked Kim, "Are you gonna take him in?" "Yep!" Kim answered, amused. "He seems to have a profound interest."

"Bryan, I hope you enjoy our club," Carol said. "This being Bryan's first time here, I'm gonna let you guys in at no charge—just sign the register. Don't say anything, okay? Jerry gets a little upset if I let people in without paying." Actually, Carol thought Bryan was an eye-catcher and wouldn't have charged him anyway, but she'd never let Kim know that.

"Thanks," Kim replied.

"By the way," Carol continued, her attitude a little more subdued, "you know Alice, don't you?"

Kim thought for a second. "Yeah, I think I know her—she's one of the assistant managers, right?"

"Yeah. Well, last week a lady named Pat Howard came in with her sub-boy and she broke almost every rule in the club. Alice was on duty and interrupted her session to put things right. She did the right thing, but she carried it way too far—she was rude and very cynical toward Pat. So Pat complained to Jerry, and Jerry told Alice she'd either be fired or have to spend two hours with Pat and Mack in the back room apologizing. They just went back. I think you might find it interesting."

Kim and Bryan signed the register. Carol pressed a little button on her desk, the door lock buzzed, and they entered.

Bryan was delighted to see all sorts of bondage furniture in the room. There were spanking benches all over the place and just about everything else a good dungeon should have. It reminded him of Nick's place, but this was ten times the size.

People were engaged in all types of BDSM play; most of the spanking benches were in use with some very lovely naked women chained to them. Another woman was chained to the back wall by her wrists and ankles, being flogged by her master.

To their right, he saw a beautiful naked young woman with her wrists cuffed in front of her and hooked to an "O" ring attached to a heavy cable that hung from a pulley in the ceiling. Bryan followed the length of the cable from the pulley to an electric winch on the wall. Standing beside her was a large half-naked man, dressed in black leather chaps and boots. Bryan watched as the man tested the connection of the ring to the cable and the woman's cuffed wrists.

"That's Alice," said Kim, pointing to the woman. "Let's sit down, I want to see this." They found two chairs against the wall a short distance from the pair. "Be very quiet," Kim whispered in Bryan's ear. "We don't want to interrupt them."

As Bryan eased down in the chair beside Kim, he noticed an older but nonetheless attractive lady sitting against the opposite wall who seemed to be supervising the scene. He realized this must be Pat. "Spread her legs, Mack, and use that long spreader bar," she said firmly.

Mack attached the ankle cuffs to Alice's ankles and connected them to the bar, spreading her legs as far apart as her body would allow and displaying the lips of her pussy opened wide. Then Pat touched a button and the winch engaged, pulling Alice's hands and arms up over her head. Alice's body was stretched as far as it could go, but her head still hung down, her long brown hair covering her face and most of her chest.

"Mack, put her hair in a ponytail and tie it to the 'O' ring," the woman said. Bryan could see a sadistic look on Mack's face that he knew all too well; Mack was enjoying this. He took a thin white rope and tied up Alice's hair, then attached the rope to the ring above her head tight enough to pull her head up and expose her neck. Her head now faced forward and her breasts jutted out from her chest, nipples pointed and hard.

"Use the red ball gag, but don't blindfold her. I want to see those sluttish eyes of hers."

When Mack picked up the gag and held it to Alice's mouth, she twisted and shook her head as much as she could. She seemed desperately frightened of the gag. "No! No!" she screamed, piercing the already loud noise in the room. "I'm not letting you put that damn thing in my mouth!" Whack! Mack's riding crop ripped across her ass, and she screamed again in genuine pain.

After that, Alice closed her eyes and obediently opened her mouth. A red welt appeared on her ass as Mack inserted the gag beyond her front teeth and buckled it behind her head.   Bryan noticed the small amount of drool that slid down Alice's chin from behind the gag. From the smile on Pat's face, Bryan could tell she saw it too.

She pressed the button again and the cable retracted upward, suspending Alice's body a foot above the floor, held only by her wrists and hair. Bryan could see the tortured strain in Alice's face. As a practiced sadist, he could appreciate the strange and mysterious feeling of helplessness this woman was enduring.

The older woman surveyed the naked beauty, then ordered, "Mack, chain the ankle spreader bar to the floor. I don't want her moving around much.

Every damn time you strike her with that whip, I want her to feel it." It was plain to see this lady meant business.

Mack took a small length of chain and snapped it to a small hook in the middle of the bar, then hooked the other end to another hook in the floor. He pulled the chain tight. Alice's body was stretched to the limit between her wrists and the ankle spreader bar, her breasts and nipples pushing up and out with her labored breathing, now completely helpless to Mack's whip. Her beautiful pussy was even more open than before, the folds of pussy skin twitching from the strain.

Bryan watched as Pat got up from her chair and slowly walked in front of them, never taking her eyes off this beautiful helpless woman. She put her lips to Alice's ear and said loud enough for all of them to hear, "My dear haughty bitch Alice, you know you were wrong to embarrass me the way you did, and when this is over I think you'll agree."

She walked by Bryan and Kim again, and Bryan noticed a hint of a smile on her face. He knew she had done it on purpose. Kim didn't notice Pat's smile, however; she was concentrating on Alice's nude body.

"Okay, Mack," Pat said, "let's start off with the flogger on that lovely back of hers."

Mack picked up the large whip, whirled it in the air, and struck a massive blow.

"*Ugh!*" Alice groaned from behind the gag as her body jerked forward from the contact. Over and over the whip fell, tormenting Alice's lean and muscular back. Mack alternated his calculated strokes to include her ass and shoulders, producing tiny red marks. After several minutes of this, her backside looked like she had just stepped out of a tanning bed. Sweat poured from her face and she squeezed her eyes shut, trying to handle the pain.

The older woman was not pleased. "Dear bitch Alice, I do suggest you open those eyes of yours," she said. "I want to see the pain in them. *NOW*!" Alice blinked, but obeyed, opening her pain-struck eyes. "Now the front, Mack!" Pat commanded.

The flogger fell across Alice's breasts and her chest pumped back and forth from the whip's torturous contact as her nipples danced to each stroke. Mack concentrated on the front of her body with military precision.

Stroke after stroke, Alice's body jerked and muffled screams and whimpers escaped her mouth. Her legs were wide apart, her pussy lips and inner thighs prominently displayed, and they received several blows. Her entire body was aflame from the punishing strokes. Red whip marks crossed her front.

"Her pussy, Mack!" Pat cried. "Do her pussy! I want to see more strokes on her pussy. *Hard*, Mack! Damn it, Mack, don't hold back, and make it hard."

Mack adjusted his position for the next contact with the flogger. A swift, penetrating direct hit to the open folds of her pussy heightened the attack.

"*Shhhhhhhhi—!*" Alice screamed desperately through the gag. Her body quivered from the tormenting stroke.

Mack continued with more strokes that cut deeper and deeper into her womanhood. Her pussy lips stood at attention like gladiators ready to do battle against overwhelming odds. The leather cuffs cut deep into her wrists. Her hands clenched, trying to reach down into the depths of her soul to find the strength to battle the penetrating sting of the whip.

Bryan stole a quick glance at Kim. She was completely lost in Alice's reactions, and he suspected she was familiar with the pain Alice was feeling.

The whipping continued for several long minutes until Alice's body was just as red in front as in back. Then Pat said, "Okay, Mack, hold up a minute." She walked over to Alice and stroked her cheek, wiping away the tears. Then she unbuckled and removed the gag. Alice took a deep breath, more tears running down her face.

Smiling, Pat bent down and licked away the sweat between Alice's lovely breasts. She then lightly bit one of her nipples.

"*Aow!*" Alice screamed. "That hurts! Please, Mistress, no more."

"My dear lovely Alice," Pat said, gazing deeply into her delicate eyes, "do you have something you want to tell me?"

Alice gasped, "Yes, ma'am! Yes, ma'am! I am so very, very sorry I acted the way I did. I'll never do it again, I assure you. Please, no more. I beg you, please, can't this be enough?"

"I think you mean what you say," Pat told Alice. "I'm just not totally convinced of your sincerity."

She put her hand between Alice's legs and inserted a finger. Alice's eyes and mouth opened, but she said nothing. Bryan could see Pat's finger slowly moving in and out of Alice's pussy.

Kim watched with a haunting fascination. Alice was lost in another world, a private world, somewhere in a sexual climate only she knew. Bryan knew the look; he had seen it before with some of his subs.

"Yes, that's just what I expected," Pat said. "You're as wet as you can be down there. Just a regular little slut, aren't we?" She pulled her finger out and licked it, tasting the womanly juices. "Not bad. A little pleasure with your pain makes for such an enlightening experience, don't you think?"

Pat reinserted the gag in Alice's mouth; this time, she accepted the gag without hesitation. Pat buckled it in place and returned to her seat. Bryan noticed another faint smile as she passed by, although she never looked at them. Kim was still transfixed by Alice's nude form.

"Mack, use the small whip on her front, the one with the two leads, and take more time on her nipples. I just love the way they dance."

Mack took only seconds to land the first of several strokes. "*Ahug!*" Alice cried out, trying to bear the torment from the whip. Her chest heaved back and forth, and sweat streamed down her cleavage. Mack increased the force of the strokes, and Alice's body continued to jerk after each stroke.

She had lost control of her body and mind. Bryan looked at Pat, and it was evident that she also had plunged even deeper into an incredible sexual state of mind.

Kim grabbed Bryan's hand and held on tight, emotions beginning to stir in her as well. Bryan was a little surprised that Kim was so involved with what they were watching, but he had to admit that this was a fabulous display.

All of a sudden, Alice stopped jerking and fell still, her eyes closed. "Hold on, Mack," said Pat, standing up. "I think she's unconscious. Would you look at that?" She calmly walked to the water cooler in the corner of the room, retrieved a cup of cold water, and poured it over Alice's head. The cold water cascaded down her face, onto her chest, and ran down her body to her pussy hair.

Alice jerked and tried to scream. "*Shiiiii!*" was all that came out.

"Well, my dear," Pat said pleasantly, "welcome back to our little world. Mack, you know it works every time." She removed the gag again. "Let me hear you apologize again, this time with a little more feeling."

Alice closed her jaws slowly, trying to relieve the ache. She gulped in air before she spoke. "Yes, ma'am! Yes, yes, ma'am! I'm so very, very sorry for what I said and did. I beg your forgiveness. I promise, *promise*, it will never happen again."

Pat reached between Alice's legs again and inserted her finger into her pussy, bringing another gasp from Alice. "Splendid, my dear. Not only do I forgive you, but you will now be one of my slaves. I will have you when and where I want. Do you understand me?" "Yes, yes, ma'am, I understand. I'll do anything you ask," Alice said. She was indeed a sex slave now.

Pat removed her finger and lightly kissed Alice's lips. Alice responded for the first time with a passionate return kiss.

"Damned right you'll do what I tell you. Okay, Mack, she's had enough. Give her a few minutes and take her down."

Pat walked back to her seat, picked up her pocketbook, and turned toward the door. Then she stopped in front of Bryan and Kim, leaned down, and gave Kim a penetrating look. "If you don't take good care of this great-looking hunk of man here, that could be you hanging up there. As incredibly pretty as you are, I'd really like to see that. I'd use the whip myself."

Kim stared at her in shock and said nothing. The older woman straightened up and patted Bryan on the shoulder. "You're a very handsome man. She's lucky to have you. If she doesn't take good care of you, give me a call and I'll put her up there like Alice." She winked at him, turned, and started towards the

door.

A few steps away, Jerry the owner stopped her. "Are you okay with this, Pat? I watched your session from the other side of the room."

"Yes. I'm fine with her. She still works for you, but from now on, her sex is mine. You may have to give her a few days off from time to time."

"Works for me," Jerry said.

Bryan and Kim left the club in silence and walked to the car. It was a while before Kim finally spoke. "Bryan, I was totally shocked by what that lady said. I've seen her in the club before, but I've never talked to her. Just remember, what you saw and heard could get me in a lot of trouble. I'm not supposed to take a visitor to a place like this."

"Kim, I'll let you in on a little secret about myself," said Bryan. "Back home, I belong to a group that does this same thing. I've seen all this before in one way or another. I understand, and don't worry; I don't talk out of school."

"Thanks." Kim seemed relieved that he so understanding. "You'll have to tell me more about your special friends back home," she said with a little smirk on her face.

"I'd like to," he answered. Kim's remarks and the day's activities had been very surprising. He could tell things were going on that he wasn't aware of, but his prospects for the future seemed quite high.

That night, Kim and Bryan met just before seven and walked to the restaurant to meet the others. Dinner went well, and everyone seemed to have a good time. Bill told Bryan that they would contact him the following week.

"Thank you, sir, I have enjoyed being here and I look forward to hearing from you," Bryan answered.

"Well, Bryan, everyone has left us, would you like to get a drink with me?" Kim asked. "I've got to check on Kelly and Peggy—they're tending bar at the old club again tonight."

"Sure, let's go." They made their way across the parking lot to the old, dark medieval-looking building and up the side steps to a large door marked "Level One." Inside, they passed through an open double door into a lounge area.

The place was a lot larger than Bryan had thought from looking at the outside of the building. A bar jutted out from the wall halfway through the room. Several people were sitting around sipping drinks, but they easily found an empty table.

Peggy walked up with a silver tray in her hand. "What can I get you guys?"

"A vodka tonic would be fine for me," Kim answered.

"And you, Bryan?"

He hesitated a second. "Bourbon and Coke on the rocks." His eyes were fixed on the silver tray. It was decorated with a pair of handcuffs encircling two glasses and a small whip that stretched around the edges of the tray.

"Great, be right back." Peggy turned and walked away. Bryan watched Peggy's long, slender legs and majestic ass as she moved gracefully across the floor toward the bar.

"Down, boy." Kim lightly touched his arm.

"Well, the way she's dressed makes you take a second look, you know?"

Bryan continued staring. The short black bikini bottoms that just covered Peggy's ass cheeks and the leather halter top that exposed most of her glamorous breasts left little to the imagination. She also wore a locked black leather collar with a small "O" ring attached in front, and a leather leash with a small chain fell from the collar to a wide belt around her waist. There were leather cuffs around each wrist and ankle. "She's a very lovely woman."

Kim let him get an eyeful, then answered his question before he could ask it. "We dress like this from time to time if there's a party going on downstairs. Level Two is where all the private parties are—invitation only."

Nick's Social (Chapter 6)

Kim was true to her word; Bryan made his flight and touched down late Sunday afternoon as scheduled. When he got home, he phoned Sally but she had not returned from her trip. He left a message, then lay down across his bed and fell asleep.

When Bryan arrived at the office the following morning, his phone rang and it was Sally. "Bryan, sorry for not calling you last night. It was really late when Sara and I got back."

"I understand. I was asleep," he replied.

"I know it was a long flight. Anyway, you've got a call on line two—a Nick Baxter."

"Thanks. I'll talk to you later." Bryan clicked over to line two. "Hi, Nick, it's been too long. How are you?"

"Hi yourself, buddy! I'm doing fine, but those guys in New York just couldn't get it together. We took a break for a couple of weeks. I'm at home now and I've talked to a few of the couples in the group. We're gonna have a little get together at my place this weekend and I want you to come. I'll do some grilling, and after that, we'll move it downstairs to the basement."

"I wouldn't miss it for the world. Can I bring a friend?"

Nick chuckled. "I don't know, can you?"

Bryan returned the laugh. "You know, I was at your place checking on things and I wasn't by myself."

"I know you were here. I hope you cleaned the basement furniture when you left?"

"You know I did." Bryan sat back in his chair. "Okay, what time will the steaks be ready?"

"Around six, and bring your friend. I'm looking forward to seeing you."

"Okay, Nick, I gotta go. See you Saturday."

Later that afternoon, Sally was arranging some papers on her desk when Bryan stepped out of his office and saw she was alone. He pulled the electric control out of his pocket and touched the "L" button. Sally almost fell out of the chair, but immediately regained her composure and glared at him. He smiled and went back into his office.

A few moments later, Sally marched into Bryan's office and stood in front of his desk, a humiliated but concerned look on her face. She kept her voice low so no one could hear. "Bryan, you've got to be more careful around here with that thing. Please! I get so damned turned on and wet down there when you do that; it makes me weak in my knees. It's embarrassing. My body is on fire and I can't do a damned thing about it. I can't concentrate on anything but having your cock in my pussy, your balls slapping against my bottom, and you whipping my ass with that damned whip." She turned and left without letting him say a word.

Bryan received the call he was waiting for on Wednesday. As always, Sally rang his extension, and he answered in his usual businesslike manner.

"Yeah, Sally."

"Got another call for you on line two," she said. "The lady said her name is Kim. It might be about that job. I hope it's good news for you—and, oh, when you get a second, I need to ask you something."

"You bet it is," he said. "Let me finish the call and then stop by my office. Patch me through." Bryan was a little nervous about this call, especially after everything that had happened that day with Kim. It was hard to think about anything else.

He heard the telephone key click. "Hello, Kim, it's Bryan," he said. "How are you?"

"I'm doing just fine, thanks for asking," she replied. "I've got Bill on hold for you—I'll talk to you later."

The phone went silent for a second, and then Bill came on the line. "Hello, Bryan!"

"Hello, Mr. Majors. How are you, sir?"

"Doing fine. I have some good news for you. After you left, Frank and I reviewed your info, and we decided we want to add you to our staff. When can you start?"

Bryan hesitated. "I need to give Mr. Samuels a couple of weeks' notice. How about the first of the month?"

"That'll do just fine. You can stay in 21 for the time being until you find a place. I'll get Kim back on the line and she can set things up for you.

Welcome aboard." The phone went silent again. The only thing Bryan could hear was his heart beating like a bass drum at a football game.

"Okay, Bryan, I'm back," said Kim. "Congratulations! It's going to be nice having you around." She seemed pleased that Bryan had accepted the job. "The first is a Monday, two weeks from now. I'll let Ray and Sam know you're coming in on that

Sunday, right?"

"That works for me." Bryan felt a lot better now that he knew he had the job.

"Great," Kim said. "See you then. Oh—thanks again for not saying anything about the tour I took you on."

"No problem, Kim. I told you I don't talk out of school. See you in two weeks."

Ten minutes later, Sally stuck her head into Bryan's office. "Hope I'm not breaking in?"

"No. It's okay. Sit down; I've got some things I need to tell you."

"I do too," she replied. "Sara and I are leaving early Saturday for the closing. Would you like to go with me? We could make a day of it. I only have two stops—there's the closing and I've got to meet the real estate agent about my new apartment."

"Do you remember the guy who gave me the movie?" Bryan asked. "I got a call from him the other day."

Sally thought for a second. "Yep, Nick Baxter. He's the guy with the great cabin and the basement of basements."

"That's right. Well, he's invited me to a party at his place Saturday night. I checked the map, and it's about an hour's drive from your new club to his place. We can get your business done and then go to his place for dinner. He's having some special friends over."

Sally's eyes opened wide and she gave him a smile. "Special friends, ha! Sounds like a setup to me. I'd love to."

The drive up on Saturday was uneventful. As they drove, Bryan and Sally talked about their new jobs and their hopes for good luck and good business. They arrived on time with all of the paperwork. Bob, the owner, seemed very excited; he would now be able to take his wife on an overdue vacation.

Bryan waited in the bar until they finished the closing. Then everyone walked out of the office and joined him for a celebratory drink. "All go well?" Bryan asked.

"You bet!" Sally replied, beaming like a light bulb. "Bob will be around for a few weeks until we get the hang of it. In any case, we take over full control on the first."

Their next stop was with the real estate agent, and the meeting went very well for Sally. She got the keys to her new place and could move in at any time.

The scenery was breathtaking as they drove cross-country to Nick's place; it was a step back in time and nature. They pulled into Nick's front yard and parked between two of the large pine trees that dotted the area. From the patio came the aroma of steaks on the grill. When Nick came over to greet them, Bryan introduced him to Sally and Nick introduced the rest of the group.

After the great meal, Nick and Bryan grabbed beers and sat down at the far end of the patio to talk about their jobs. After a while, Nick's friends Denise and Mary came over, followed by Sally.

"Nick," Denise said softly, "Mary and I want to take Sally downstairs and show her a few of the interesting things down there, if that's all right with you and Bryan?"

"Okay by me." Nick sat up in his chair and waved a hand. "But only if Bryan says it's okay."

Bryan raised his eyebrows a bit and looked at Sally, then hesitated. "Sally, you okay with this?"

"You bet." She smiled at Bryan. "It's fine."

Bryan shrugged. "Go for it, then."

"Don't worry, Bryan," Nick said as the three women headed for the basement door. "She's in good hands."

"That's what I'm afraid of," Bryan joked. He knew she was; this wasn't the first party he had been to with these women.

Sally recognized the large basement from the first time she had visited with Bryan; nothing much had changed. Denise escorted her across the dimly lit dungeon to the X-frame rack that sat at the far end of the room.

"Take your clothes off, Sally," Denise commanded. "The guys will be down soon, and we want to have a little woman-to-woman fun before they come in."

Sally had never had a sexual experience with another woman before, but she secretly craved the thrill of a woman's touch. With a little help from Denise and Mary, she undressed and stood on wobbly legs, naked except for the electric belt.

"What in heaven's name are you wearing, dear?" Denise asked, amazed at the sight of the belt.

"It's Bryan's idea, and I must say, most electrifying," Sally said, a little embarrassed.

"I bet it is, but for now, let's take this thing off." Denise started to unsnap the belt clips.

"Maybe we should ask Bryan about this first?" Mary asked, looking at Denise.

Denise's juices were already flowing at the sight of Sally's amazing nude body. All she wanted to do was take that body for a ride; she didn't give a rat's ass about the electric belt.   "When we finish with her, we'll put it back on. He'll never know," she told Mary as she removed it.

Mary buckled a leather cuff around each of Sally's wrists and fastened them to the eyebolts at the top of the rack. Denise fastened a pair of similar cuffs around her ankles and attached them to the legs of the rack.

Spread-eagled and bound to the rack, Sally could only move her pelvic area. She was filled with excitement at the idea of two women taking complete control of her. It was certainly unexpected. An old fear that had been trapped in her body was melting away, and now a mystical light was shining at the end of this whirlwind tunnel.

Then Mary wrapped a large leather belt tightly around Sally's waist and buckled it behind the rack. The belt held her fast to the frame while emphasizing her hourglass figure.

Something new and thrilling was taking place within Sally. She felt safe with these two women, but the excitement of uncertainty had her juices flowing. Her sex was aflame with desire. She needed relief—something to hold the flame down for a few minutes, at least.

Mary stood in front of Sally and stared deep into her sparkling eyes for a few seconds. Sally stared back, lost in the haunting fascination of her gaze, but said nothing. Mary inched closer, and her moist lips lightly touched Sally's lips. Sally raised her eyebrows a little at the delicious taste of another woman's lips, then accepted the sensuous kiss. I only lasted for a few seconds, but the soft, stimulating contact suggested there was a lot more to come.

"Have you ever had another woman kiss you before?" Mary asked, searching her eyes for the answer she already knew.

Sally's heart beat faster and faster. Ready to accommodate whatever Mary wanted to do, she whispered, "No, this is the first time. It feels good."

Knowing she wanted more, Mary gently lifted Sally's chin and kissed her again. This time, she forced her mouth open and their tongues played with each other for several seconds before Mary ended the kiss and moved down to Sally's chest. Sally's nipples were already hard, standing at attention like aristocratic flames of desire. Mary licked the right one first, then the left.

"Oh! That's so good. I feel so naked. Why do I feel so naked?" Sally moaned, desperate for Mary's touch.

"Hold on a minute," Denise said, watching Mary play with Sally's body like a doll. "Would you take a look at this?" Denise moved to Sally's front and eyed her crevice. "Did Bryan shave you like this?" she asked, interested in the disposition of her pubic hair.

"Yes, he did," Sally answered.

Denise spread Sally's pussy lips apart and inserted a finger deep into her pussy, feeling her wetness and heat. "*Hum!*" Sally grunted, trying to open her legs more and force the finger deeper into her pussy. She wanted to ride that finger as long as she could.

From a nearby table, Denise picked up a large vibrator that resembled a man's cock and turned it on. The hum was low, but loud enough to hear. She rubbed it between Sally's legs, slowly at first and then more quickly, up and down against her slit. The vibrator was thick and hard with a rubbery texture.

Meanwhile, Mary picked up a two-pronged whip and lightly stroked Sally's nipples and breasts. With the pleasure of the vibrator and the gentle touch of the whip, Sally was quickly moving into a zone only meant for a few. She tried to squat down to receive the vibrator; she wanted it inside her, all of it. Nothing else mattered. Beads of sweat were appearing from between her breasts.

Mary's whip found its mark again, and this time the stroke was more severe. Sally cried out and threw her head to one side. "*Aheee*! I can't stand this, fuck me, fuck me, and please fuck me! Put that thing inside me!" She yanked on her bonds, but they held fast.

Denise stopped her masturbation of Sally's pussy, put the vibrator down, and walked to the table. In a few seconds, she returned with the bright red ball gag. "Open your mouth, dear—just enough so I can get this in place."

She was a little surprised when Sally quickly obeyed her command. The gag
went into her mouth and Sally closed her eyes as Denise buckled the leather strap around her head. The blindfold was next, and now Sally could neither talk nor see what was going on.

As Denise moved away from Sally, she pinched her right nipple rather hard and pulled her breast. "*Agggg*!" Sally couldn't get much more out.

"That did the trick." Denise nodded to Mary with a smile. "We don't want the guys down here just yet, do we?"

Mary gave Sally's left breast another stroke with the whip. "*Agggg!*" A little drool eased from the gag and dribbled down Sally's chin. "I see what you mean," Mary said as her eyes roamed over Sally's body.

Denise turned the vibrator on again and slowly inserted it into Sally's vagina. At the same time, another stroke from Mary's whip found its target on Sally's right nipple. Sally had experienced pure pain and pure pleasure at the same time before, but never from two women. Their softness and cruelty were so different from Bryan's. It had to be the mysterious touch of a woman that made the difference.

After several minutes of this, Mary and Denise knew that Sally was close to having an orgasm. "Let it go, Sally. Come for me, my sweet little pet," Denise whispered. "This is for you, baby." Denise kissed her cheek as another stroke from Mary's whip found its mark.

Both women stopped their ministrations and watched Sally as her body stiffened in orgasm. Her body writhed and jerked at the same time; she was on a high, a mind trip, moaning into the gag, a slut wanting more. A few minutes

passed and her orgasm eased.

"Well, Denise," Mary said, "she looks like she's finished. Do you think she can take some more? I've got another whip for her."

"I think you and Denise have had enough fun with her," Nick said from behind them. He grabbed Mary's arm and turned her around to face him. The other two men were standing there as well.

"Here she is, Mike, she's all yours," Nick said, turning Mary over to her Master.

"Thanks, I'll take it from here." Mike pointed to the floor with the riding crop in his hand. "Mary, take your clothes off. All of them!"

Mary immediately obeyed, and in a few seconds, she was totally naked.

"Get on all fours now, and hold your head up."

She said nothing and got down on her hands and knees.

"Open your mouth," Mike ordered as he unclipped a leather collar from his belt and locked it around her neck. Then he slipped a gag into Mary's mouth beyond her front teeth and buckled it behind her head. Finally, he attached a chain to her collar. Holding the leash up, he told her, "Let's go for a very long walk. Maybe we'll take that walk to the lake." Shuddering at the thought, Mary crawled after him as he walked off.

"Well, Denise, it's your turn," Nick said, taking possession of his submissive. "Time to get those clothes of yours off." Denise stripped and Nick escorted her to the basement wall, where she would be spending a lot of time.

Bryan looked at Sally, still bound to the rack with the gag and blindfold, the vibrator humming away. "Looks like you really did it up right this time. I hope it wasn't too much for you?" Slowly, Sally shook her head, signaling that she was all right.

"Okay." Bryan chuckled. "Wait a minute, what's this?" He moved closer. "It looks like you've taken off your electric belt."

"*Noga! Noga!*" Sally shook her head, her hair flying in front of her face.

"Did Denise take your belt off without permission?" Nick asked, walking back to them.

Sally nodded her head.

"Don't worry, Bryan, I'll take it from here," Nick said.

"Works for me," Bryan answered. "I have a few things to set up, so just enjoy yourself, Sally, and I'll get you down in a few minutes." He arranged several leather belts on the floor under the hoist cable and then let Sally down from the rack.

Bryan let her rest in a chair for a few minutes, for which Sally was thankful. While she rested, he watched sweet Mary still crawling on her hands and knees, making a valiant effort to keep up with Mike. On the other side of the room, another Master was teaching his submissive the art of enjoying a hot wax bath, dripping candles over her most sensitive body parts. Bryan had noticed a very cute blonde at supper, and her bottom looked even more seductive bent over the spanking bench. Blonde hair and red ass—a nice combination. Nick's dungeon was certainly being put to the test tonight.

Denise was secured to the wall by her wrists and ankles in a spread-eagle position. Nick was attaching some clips to her nipples, and Bryan could tell they were causing real pain. That would teach Denise to ask permission before she removed any belts from someone else's submissive!

"Okay, Sally, it's your turn again." Bryan helped her up, led her over to the leather belts on the floor, and made her lie face-down across them. He took a wide leather harness shaped like a G-string and buckled it around her waist and between her legs, over the end of the vibrator. "This will keep the vibrator in place. We don't want to lose that, do we?"

He raised Sally's arms over her head, then buckled one belt above her breasts, one below her breasts, one around her stomach, one just below her ass, one around her knees, and one around her ankles. He pulled her hands and arms behind her back and used another belt to secure her wrists, palms together. A final belt secured her elbows together.

Bryan pressed the hoist button and the cable descended from the ceiling to a point just above her wrists. He attached a length of chain to each of the belts that were buckled around Sally and secured them to the big "O" ring at the end of the hoist cable.

"Sally," Bryan said, "some people call this position a classic hog-tie. I hope you enjoy it." He bent her knees, pulled her ankles up to meet her wrists, and buckled them to the ring as well. Then he pressed the hoist button again, and it lifted her into the air.

When she was four feet off the ground, Bryan stopped the hoist and admired Sally's suspension. "God, Sally, you look fabulous in that position." Her head hung down and her face was covered by her hair. The blindfold was still in place, the gag was still doing its job, and he could still hear the faint sound of the vibrator working away inside that beautiful pussy.

"You know I can do anything I want to you. You are one sexy woman," Bryan whispered in her ear.

Sally nodded her head; she understood that she was totally helpless. Her body swayed a little in her suspension as she breathed. She hoped she could handle whatever he was going to do to her. Tonight was new territory, and the anticipation of what was to come made her whole body tingle.

Bryan looked across the basement to Nick and Denise. Nick had just finished forcing Denise's legs up and securing them to her outstretched wrists. She was suspended about four feet off the floor and attached to the wall with nothing holding her ass up. Her nipple clamps were linked by a small chain that held two weights, and he could tell they were pulling her breasts and pinching her nipples hard. Her legs were wide apart, her pussy in full view, just asking to be fucked. Bryan noticed that she had no pubic hair; he wondered if Nick did the shaving.

Nick began a slow but aggressive assault with a riding crop. In a few minutes, Denise's pussy and inner legs were bright red with marks, and she was making small sounds through her gag.

Bryan looked around the dungeon and realized that everyone else had left. Only the four of them remained. It was now a private party—just what he liked.

As Nick finished whipping Denise's pussy, Bryan admired his masterful whip control. He could see the glare of sweat on Denise's upper chest. Her breasts and nipples heaved up and down as she breathed, a spectacular view of a sex slave offering her body to her master.

"I'll give her a little rest. She's gonna be up there for a while," Nick told Bryan as he crossed the room toward them. "What a lovely sight!" he said, eyeing Sally's helpless figure. "She's a beautiful woman, and man, I love that position. Wait a minute, though—I think you need to put some nipple clamps on her." Nick walked to the table, picked up a pair of adjustable clamps, and attached one to each nipple.

"*Noggg!*" Sally moaned from behind the gag.

"I also have some weights," Nick told Bryan. "What do you say, you think we should use them?"

"I like the idea, Nick," Bryan said. "Let's do it."

Nick attached a weight to each clamp and then let go.

"*Noggg!*" Sally cried again.

"There, that's better," said Nick. "One other thing, Bryan. Take this little rope and tie it around the gag strap buckle at the back of her head."

Bryan complied.

"Okay, now lift her head so it's straight with her body."

Bryan put his hand under Sally's chin and eased her head up, then tied the rope to the hoist cable to fix her head in that position.

"Thanks, Nick. I love the look."

"She's a beautiful woman, Bryan." Nick seemed pleased with the added clamps and her new look. Bryan was enjoying the additions as well.

"Yep, she loves the attention," Bryan said. "Well, Nick, everyone has gone, so I guess we should too?"

"Before we go, let me do something else to Denise. Come on." They walked back to where Denise was suspended against the wall with her pussy in plain view. "Bryan, look on that table and bring me that little white box." Bryan gave Nick the box. He opened it and pulled out two adjustable metal clamps.

"They look like nipple clamps," Bryan said.

"These, my friend, are pussy lip clamps. Watch!" Nick adjusted the tension on the first clamp, then pinched Denise's left pussy lip and attached the clamp.

"*Nogagg!*" Denise cried, shifting her body to handle the pain. Bryan could tell the clamp was tight. Next, Nick attached a piece of string to the clamp and tied it around her leg, pulling her pussy open even more.

"*Nogagg!*" Denise gurgled from behind the gag when the second clamp went on. Her entire body shook as Nick tied the other clamp around her right thigh. Both of her pussy lips were now stretched open.

"My word, Nick," Bryan said. "Would you look at that? You can see inside her entire cunt."

Nick handed Bryan the two-pronged leather whip. "Denise, my dear little slave," he said, "as a sadistic Master, I'm gonna let Bryan lay twelve strokes on that gorgeous pussy of yours. This is for taking off Sally's belt without asking permission. Bryan, make them good ones."

At Bryan's first stroke, the sound of leather hitting female flesh echoed throughout the room and the shriek from Denise's gagged mouth shocked both men. "*Ahee! Ahee!*" Denise did a good job of getting some noise around the gag. After five more strokes, red lines appeared on Denise's clit. The more he hit her, the more violent he got. It was almost addictive.

"Get inside her, Bryan," Nick instructed him. "She needs to feel this."

On Bryan's next stroke, the leather thongs disappeared into Denise's vagina. "*UGH! UGH!*" Her body jerked and she shook her head violently. Sweat glistened over her entire body as he completed the remaining strokes. She moaned and gasped for air from behind the gag.

"Okay, that's enough," Nick said. "I think she got the message. Didn't you, my dear?" Denise nodded several times.

Bryan laid the whip down on a nearby table. "What do we do next about the girls?"

"I guess we can let them go in the morning," Nick sighed. "What do you say we get a beer?"

"Sounds great," Bryan agreed. "I just have one more thing to do to Sally." He reached his hand between Sally's legs and turned the vibrator control to the high position. The hum grew in intensity, and both men could easily hear the sound of the vibrator deep inside Sally's body. "*Noggg! Noggg!*" Sally tried to scream.

"Sally dear, Nick tells me the vibrator Denise used has some heavy-duty batteries in it. They could keep going all night," Bryan said, putting his hand on her ass cheek and feeling the vibration.

"They don't need the light," Nick said. He switched the light off and both men started up the stairs. "I think I just may have to check out that bar and club of Sally's."

The Clients (Chapter 7)

"You up?" Nick yelled, knocking on the bedroom door.

Bryan was already awake, showered, and dressed. "Sure am," he answered, tucking his shirt into his shorts and opening the door.

"I'll fix us a nice breakfast if you go down and let the girls loose," Nick declared.

"You got a deal," Bryan agreed. "It may take a few minutes, so don't hurry with breakfast."

He knew it was going to take some time for the women to get their sea legs back; being restrained for an extended period of time has an effect on the body.

Bryan opened the door to the basement and turned the light on. Both women shifted a bit in their bondage at the noise. He went to Denise first, let her down, and removed all the restraints. For the first time in over eight hours, she was completely free of bondage. She sat on the floor, her head hanging down, and didn't utter a word.

Next, he activated the hoist and lowered Sally to the floor. He removed the belts and straps that held her in place, the blindfold, and then the ball gag. Her body shook as the nipple clamps and weights came off; her nipples and breasts were ever so sensitive to his touch.

"*Aow*! That hurts!" Sally gasped. He eased his hand between her legs and slid the vibrator from the depths of her pussy. It was still humming along, just as he had expected. Sally let out another gasp of air at the removal, then lay still for several minutes.

"Ladies, the Jacuzzi is ready," Nick said, entering the basement with coffee in hand. "Clean up and I've got a fabulous breakfast for us all." The mention of breakfast seemed to help the situation, and things started to get back to normal.

Soon after breakfast, Bryan and Sally said goodbye to Nick and Denise and got back into the car to head home.

"Bryan, you seem rather quiet," Sally said, sensing there might be something wrong. "Is something bothering you? Want to talk about it?"

"Well—" He hesitated. "Yes, I do. Tell me about last night. How do you feel about what happened?"

"I've never been suspended before, ever." Sally adjusted her handcuffed hands a little and shifted her strapped body in the car seat. This was going to take some time.

"The strain on my body was so intense it was overwhelming. I can't tell you how many times I almost lost control. It was haunting. No matter how I tried to move, I couldn't change my position. That vibrator and those nipple clamps never surrendered, no matter how I turned. I knew you would let me go eventually, but it made me feel like I was going to be there forever. I wanted to please you, and I know you wanted to push my limits. I was afraid

I couldn't stay like that all night, but I know you only wanted me to experience something new."

"I noticed you came several times during the night." Bryan was glad she felt good about her experience.

"My God, yes!" Sally said. "A completely helpless feeling washed over me so many times, and my body responded to it so strongly that I had one orgasm right after another.

When you let me down, I was totally drained. Right now, I'm the most sexually satisfied that I have ever been."

"What about your experience with Mary and Denise? I'm sure that was something different."

"Mary kissed me a couple of times. No other woman has ever kissed me like that. It was strange, but it was so exciting, tender, and loving. Just her touch started my juices flowing, and all I could think about was her putting something in my cunt." Sally paused and laughed. "Listen to me! My mouth has really gone south, you know?"

"I had a good time too." Bryan smiled. "You are a truly gorgeous woman, and when you're in bondage, your beauty reaches a new level. I can't explain why that is, but it's the truth."

"Thank you, kind sir. You are most gracious to say that."

When they arrived at Bryan's house, Sally said she would see him at work on Monday. She waved and drove off. Bryan hit the "L" button on the electric belt and she waved again. He chuckled.

The final Friday came, and Bryan and Sally arrived at work with their cars loaded, each pulling a carryall trailer. Mr. Samuels gave them their paychecks and bonuses, wished them well, and said goodbye.

They left the building, walked across the parking lot to the picnic table, and kissed for several seconds. The kiss was an embodiment of pleasure, almost a ritual.

"Bryan," Sally said, "you have been a star in my dull life and unlocked doors that I've hidden since college. I never expected we would do the things together that we've done. You have made many of my fantasies come true, and for that, I'll never forget you. Please keep in touch with me; you have my address."

"I'm truly going to miss you, Sally," Bryan said, holding back his emotions and looking deeply into her sparkling eyes. "A man can get lost in those eyes of yours. It's hard to explain, but your eyes tell so much about how special you really are. No matter what else is going on, those eyes are a treasure. Like you." He paused, then continued, "I'm trying to move up to a new level in my life, and I have you to thank for it. You have given me inspiration to move ahead, and words cannot explain my gratitude."

She smiled and said nothing else, but reached up, gave him a quick kiss, and got into her car.

"I have something for you, before you leave," Bryan said as he pulled out the little electric control box from his jacket pocket and gave it to her. "Make sure you cut it off when you're not using it. The batteries will last longer."

"Thanks, I'll try to remember that," Sally said. Their eyes met. They knew their time was over and a new life was ahead for both of them, but it was still hard to say goodbye.

Bryan watched as she drove out of the parking lot, around the corner, and out of his life. He turned back toward the office building where he had worked since college and shook his head. It was a little sad to leave. The leaves of the oak tree outside his old office window rustled in a slight breeze. "Onward and upward," he said to nobody. He got into his car and drove out of the parking lot into a new life.

Sunday evening, Bryan turned his car off the main road, drove into the Windsor Shades entrance, and stopped at the guard station. Ray appeared from the building door as he had the first time Bryan visited.

"Hi, Ray, remember me? Bryan Wescott."

"Oh, yes! Hi, Mr. Wescott, I've been expecting you. Hope you had a good trip? Mr. Majors said you should be coming in today. Let me get you your car tag."

Ray returned from the guard station with the tag. "From now on, put this tag on the driver's side of the car so we can see it. You can use the outside lane and you won't have to stop for whoever is on duty. See Sam at the office; he has your key to 21."

"Thanks, it was a great trip," Bryan said. "I'll see you later." He was tired, and all he wanted to do was get some much-needed rest.

After getting the keys from Sam and finding his parking place, he opened the door to number 21. There was a letter on the table: "I put food and drinks in the refrigerator. Bill said to call the office on Monday, but take the day off to get unpacked. Kim."

Bryan fell asleep on the couch.

He reported to work on Tuesday, as requested, and Bill introduced him to Tim Collins and Jack Springer. "Tim here is responsible for training new people on our paper trail and Jack handles the money transfers. These are two very important people for the company."

Bill introduced Bryan to the rest of the staff, then led him to his new office. "It's not as big as you might like, but I think it'll do for now." He gave Bryan the office key and told him to look around.

After checking out his new office and getting things together, Bryan met with Tim to learn the procedures. For the next few weeks, he made great progress in the new job and getting to know his co-workers.

Early one Wednesday morning, Bryan's office phone rang. "I need you to come to my office," Bill said. "I've got a client for you."

Bryan walked into Bill's office a few minutes later. A woman was sitting there with Bill, and she looked familiar.

"Close the door," said Bill. "Bryan, I would like to introduce you to Pat

Howard. Pat, this is Bryan Wescott. He is new to our staff, but I think he can get you on the right foot with a very good investment plan."

Pat raised her eyebrows and studied Bryan's face as they shook hands. "Haven't we met before? You look very familiar."

"I don't think so," Bryan said. "I'm new to the area." Bryan knew where he had seen her before, but he didn't let on. Visions of the Castaway Club raced through his mind, where he had seen her with the woman named Alice. Pat was a striking woman in many ways and not easily forgotten. He remembered how demanding she had been at the club and her desire to punish Alice.

"Here's her file, Bryan. Take her to your office and get things started."

This was the third time Pat had met with Bill, but she had not yet decided to make an investment. Bill knew she had the money, but there was something missing. He hoped that this new approach would persuade her to invest with the firm.

Bryan and Pat left Bill's office and walked by the front desk on the way to Bryan's office. As Pat passed the desk, she noticed Kim typing away at the computer. Kim glanced up, but didn't say anything. Pat smiled and continued to follow Bryan.

She eased into the lounge chair in Bryan's office. "I know where I've seen you now," Pat said. "You and that cute little subby at the computer were at the Castaway Club some time back, and you watched me correct a problem I had with Alice."

Bryan sat down behind his desk, put the file down, and studied her face. He remembered Alice's beautiful naked suspended body and those fantastic red marks Mack had applied to her skin. It had been a spectacular session. "How is Alice doing these days?" he asked. "I remembered you, but I didn't want to say anything in front of Bill. Kim wasn't supposed to take me there. As she put it, it wasn't part of the tour. I was here for an interview, and she was just showing me the town."

Pat knew Bryan was a player, but she wasn't sure how much, or in what way. She decided to test the waters. "Alice is now completely in my stable, but I have had some problems with her," Pat said. "She will suck a man's cock—and do a good job—but for some reason, she won't swallow his cum."

"Well, little lady," Bryan said, "I might just have a answer for a problem like that. I'll have to make up a little device for you—that is, if you're interested?"

Pat seemed puzzled. "What kind of contraption do you have that will make her do that?"

"Let me work on it and I'll get back to you," said Bryan.

"I look forward to seeing it. Let me know when you have it finished."

"Could you tell me more about this stable thing?" Bryan asked.

"Yes, that's right, my stable," Pat said with a glint in her eye. "I have two submissive men and three submissive women, including Alice. They service my needs on a very regular basis. Every other day, one of them will show up at my basement dungeon and the games will begin."

"I bet you have some interesting contests for your group," Bryan said, sitting back in his chair.

"They play a lot of fetch," Pat said. "Well, Mr. Wescott, I take it you're dominant—or have I misread something here?"

"Dom," Bryan answered without hesitation. "Always have been and always will be."

"Have you had a session with that cute little subby out front yet? I think they call her Kim. You do know she's incredibly submissive, right? I've seen her at the club with those other two women out front. I've also seen her in some very torturous sessions. Some of the Doms at the club have remarked about how submissive she is. It appears that not only does she love being tied up, but she takes the whip quite well."

Bryan wasn't sure how to answer. "We haven't done anything yet, but I'm working on it."

"Are you sure you're not submissive at all?" Pat asked. "You know, you could be my third sub boy. You're a very handsome man, and I bet we could have a great time together. Just think what it would be like to have me sitting on your beautiful back holding a leash attached to a beautiful leather collar around that neck of yours."

"No, thank you." Bryan coughed. "I'm a top and I enjoy that role. I love to play with young, attractive submissive women and watch their reactions. It's just the way I am."

"Okay, I guess, for now. Maybe I'll find out something different one of these days," Pat said.

"Maybe you will, but for now, let's get to your money."

"Straight to the point," she said. "I like that in a man."

"What do you do for a living Pat? Bill left out that part on your form."

"Well—" She paused. "I own five ice cream stores, and I sell a lot of ice cream. I have three stores in town, one in the next city south of here, and the other north of town."

"So much for a vanilla life, I guess," Bryan joked, shrugging his shoulders.

Pat laughed. "And you have a sense of humor! I like that. I'm also a part owner of the Castaway Club."

"So that's why you could punish Alice that way. I wondered about that."

"That's right. No one else knows; I'm what you call a silent partner. I gave Jerry a lot of money for that place. We do really well, you know."

"I bet you do," Bryan said. He paused to flip through her file. "I want to set you up with six companies, add some insurance, and reinvest the dividends."

Pat seemed ready to do business. "Okay, I have a check here for twenty thousand. Let's start with that and see how it goes. If we do well, I'll put in another two hundred and fifty thousand."

"Stop by next week to sign the final papers, and I'll get things started," Bryan said, shaking her hand.

Bryan felt comfortable talking to Pat about both business and personal things, and she was his first client. Things were looking up!

As Pat walked by the front desk on her way out, she winked at Kim, who was still at the computer. Kim knew who Pat was. She had seen her at the Castaway many times. She could only imagine what she might have told Bryan.

Later that day, Bill asked Bryan to come back to his office.

"What's up, Bill?" Bryan asked as he walked in.

"You did real good with Pat this morning," Bill said. "I'm proud of you. I wasn't sure how long it would take to get her to invest. Jack told me you gave him her check and all the forms were correct. I thought she would invest more."

"Don't worry about that." Bryan smiled. "She said that if things go right, she would up the kitty to two hundred and fifty thousand."

"Great! I knew we picked the right man for the job." Bill slapped Bryan on the back. Then the office door opened. "Here's Kelly and Mr. Ling. Thanks, Kelly, for picking up Mr. Ling."

"No problem." Kelly pulled the door shut as she left.

"Mr. Chi Ling, this is Bryan Wescott. He's our international investment counselor. Bryan, Mr. Chi Ling."

"Nice to meet you, sir." Bryan took his cue from Bill and put his best foot forward.

"Nice met you, Miser Bryan." Ling's English was not very good.

"Mr. Ling is the CEO of a car parts company in Japan," Bill continued. "He and his four partners are very interested in American investments. However, he has run into some problems with his co-investors. I would like you to take his file and see what changes can be made. We can meet on Friday and go over things again. That should give you some time to work on it." Bill looked at Ling. "Is that okay with you, Mr. Ling?"

"No problem. Miser Bill," Ling said. "Me look forward see new changes. Miser Bill, we go your club Saturday night?"

"You bet, Mr. Ling." Bill looked at Bryan. "There's a private party Saturday night at the Club, but before we go, I'd like to have a drink in the main bar if you can make it. Say around six. You know where the front door is; just push the button and Kim will let you in."

"I'd love to," Bryan responded. "Mr. Ling, sir, it's my pleasure to meet you. If I'm going to make these changes, I have to get to work."

"Nice met you, Miser Bryan." They shook hands.

"I should be on time," Bryan said to Bill, "but I have a meeting with a real estate lady in the early afternoon. Margaret Lewis is going to show me a house at Pikes Point."

"That's a nice area. We'll see you then. Tell Kelly Mr. Ling is ready to go. He's staying in number 24 at the townhouses, just a few steps from you."

"Maybe I'll see you later then, Mr. Ling?" Bryan asked, turning to leave.

"That nice, Miser Bryan, maybe so."

Level Two (Chapter 8)

Bill and Bryan met with Mr. Ling on Friday as planned. He was pleased with Bryan's changes to the investments; Bryan had added new incentives, a few new potential growth companies, and a larger insurance plan for the investors' families, as well as several new ways of reinvesting the dividends. Bill took a close look at the file and was happy with the changes. Even Frank got in a few words about some of the investment potential.

After Mr. Ling had left the meeting, Bryan asked, "What kind of money, Bill? Has this been worth it?"

"About five million. A nice piece of change, don't you think?" Bill said.

Bryan clicked his heels and held his chin up proudly as he walked out of Bill's office.

Early Saturday afternoon, as planned, Bryan met with Margaret Lewis from Lewis Real Estate. As they drove down the gravel road toward the house she was showing him, Bryan couldn't help noticing how secluded the place was. It reminded him of Nick Baxter's house in the middle of nowhere. A few trees in the yard offered plenty of shade, and the view overlooking the point was breathtaking.

The tour of the house ended in the basement. Margaret Lewis turned the light on at the head of the steps beside the kitchen door and they descended to a basement door. She opened the closed door and turned another light on to display a large empty room.

Bryan was intensely pleased with the basement room; it was even larger than Nick's dungeon, and the ceiling was a little higher than usual. He spent a long time browsing around in the barren basement room. "Just right," he thought, looking at the beams in the ceiling. "Nice place for a suspension hoist." He wondered if the realtor knew what he was thinking.

"I don't know much about basements, but this looks like a dungeon," she suggested.

"It sure does," Bryan said without thinking. "There's a lot of room down here. I guess you could do most anything you wanted to and not be disturbed."

Margaret turned her head and shrewdly glanced at Bryan. "That's an interesting take on it. I guess you're right, though; as isolated as this place is, I don't think anybody would bother you."

She continued her detailed description of the place. "This house belonged to an older couple, but the husband died and the wife has been in poor health. She moved to Chicago with her daughter and put us in charge of selling it. The asking price is two hundred seventy-five thousand. Thirty-five down, about 6.5% interest. Payments will run about fifteen hundred a month with insurance and taxes."

"Little out of my league right now, but I do like the house," Bryan told her, trying to figure how he could make it work.

"Take your time. The place has been vacant for about a year now. I don't think it will sell any time soon. Most people don't like the isolation." Margaret was trying to offer Bryan a ray of hope.

Afterwards, Bryan drove back to the Club to have the drink Bill had promised. He pressed the button at the upstairs entrance and Kim's angel voice responded, "May I help you?"

Bryan bent down and spoke into the box. "It's me, Kim—Bryan." The door buzzed, and he pushed it open and walked down the hall to the bar.

A voice called from one side of the room. "Over here, Bryan!" Bryan glanced in the direction of the voice and saw Bill seated at a large table with Frank, Mr. Ling, and two lovely ladies. They watched as he made his way through the maze of tables. "Have a seat, Bryan," Bill said. "This is Virginia and this is Amy. You know everyone else."

"Ladies, it's nice to meet you," Bryan said. "Gentlemen, nice to see you again." He sat down next to Bill.

Peggy, who was working as hostess and waitress for the night, came over to take their drink order. Bryan couldn't help noticing her outfit as she started back toward the bar. She was wearing the same large black collar with a "O" ring that he had seen the first time he was there, held in place by a tiny suitcase-style lock. Similar locks held black leather cuffs on each of her wrists and ankles. A leash hung down from the collar and was tied to a large black leather belt just above her black bikini bottoms. A small black pouch was attached to the belt as well. Her breasts looked firm and soft under a short black leather halter top that barely covered her nipples. The bikini bottoms were closer to a thong and only covered the crack of her ass, leaving her ass cheeks fully exposed—a pleasant sight for Bryan to watch as she glided across the room to the bar.

"Looks really nice, doesn't it?" Bill grinned at Bryan.

"I should say so." Bryan continued to stare.

"When we have a private party like this one, the girls try to get in the mood, if you know what I mean."

"I can certainly see that," Bryan replied, catching sight of Kim at the bar in a similar outfit. "They're very beautiful women."

After a few minutes, Peggy came back with the drinks. "Where's Kelly?" Bill asked. "I thought she was working with the two of you tonight."

"She's here, Bill," Peggy said. "She just stepped down to Level Two for a few minutes to see a guy she's been dating. You might know him—Ted Darling?"

Bill sat back in his chair and thought for a second. "He's one of the guys who sets up the parties and helps on Level Three," he said.

"You got it." Peggy turned and started away.

Bryan just had to say something. "I love the outfit, Peggy," he called after her.

She turned around with a smirk. "Thanks," she said, then continued toward the bar with a little more wiggle in her walk.

Soon, Frank left and the others went to attend the party downstairs. It was a members-only party and Bryan wasn't a member, so he moved over to the bar and started to talk to Kim. Then Kelly came in with a frown on her face and sat down beside him. Kim and Bryan could both see that she was upset about something.

"Kelly, do you want to talk about it?" Kim asked.

Kelly sighed a bit and took a deep breath, frowning as if there was some external force ready to make her explode. "You know that guy Ted Darling?" she said angrily, then continued without waiting for an answer. "Well, he has some cute redhead bitch in the corner, and I guess he'll have her clothes off in a little while and be spanking the hell out of her ass."

"He's the guy you've gone out with a few times, right?" Kim asked.

"Yep, he's the one."

"Well sometimes that's the way it goes, you know," Bryan interjected. "I guess you just have to grin and bear it—no pun intended, but I love your outfit." Kelly was sporting the same black leather that Peggy and Kim were wearing.

"I bet you do," Kelly giggled.

Kim and Bryan both laughed. "See, you feel better already," Kim said. "Look, things are slow for now, Kelly—why don't you take Bryan downstairs for a little while, show him what's going on, and try to relax a bit?"

Kelly glanced at Kim questioningly.

"It's okay, Kelly, Bryan knows what's going on. He's okay."

"Want to go?" Kelly asked, her eyebrows raised.

"I thought it was a members-only party," Bryan replied, remembering what Bill had said.

"Well, it is," Kelly said, "but I got a key."

Bryan followed this incredibly lovely woman down the back steps to a door with a lock that reminded him of a hotel door. She put a key card in the slot, the green light came on, and she opened the door.

Bryan could hear deep bass drum sounds echoing through the hall as they entered. "Sounds a little spooky," he whispered.

"It should. It's supposed to be a dungeon, you know," Kelly said. "Come on, follow me."

They went through another door into a room where a performance was going on. At the back, there was a row of empty folding chairs. "Sit down and watch, Bryan," Kelly told him.

Fifteen people were sitting in a small group watching a man on a small stage with a leather flogger in his right hand. He was dressed in nothing but a pair of leather chaps, which displayed his semi-hard cock. Bryan could hear him describing several techniques for properly using the whip on a submissive. After answering a few questions from the group, he asked his assistant to join him on stage. An attractive blonde stood up from a front seat.

"My dear, if you would be so kind to remove your robe, we can proceed," the man said.

The assistant removed her robe and stood gloriously naked before the group. There was no sag in her breasts; they were a little larger than most, and looked very sensual and inviting. The nipples were hard and stood at attention. Her legs were long and muscular, and there were no signs of any tan lines on her belly. Bryan also noticed how flat her stomach was, with no signs of fat and no pubic hair. Her pussy slit was open to view. He liked that.

"Kelly, look at her slit. I think she opened her legs so everyone could see that pussy of hers." Bryan thought God had taken a little more time on that part of the woman's body.

"Quiet, Bryan!" Kelly whispered. "I don't want to interrupt this."

The Master took leather cuffs and buckled them around her wrists, pulled them over her head, and attached them to a cable in the ceiling. A few cranks with the hoist handle on the wall pulled her body taut. Her feet were still on the floor, but not by much. From his practice as a sadist, Bryan knew that this stretching would amplify the pain of a whip.

Kelly glanced at Bryan to see his reaction to the display. She was a little surprised that he seemed so comfortable with what he was watching. "She loves it. She's done this before," Kelly whispered in his ear. "You're sure you're okay with this?"

Bryan could smell Kelly's exquisite womanly odor. His cock was starting to rise, and he shifted position in the seat to avoid drawing attention to the fact. "I'll let you in on a little secret," he whispered back. "I was in a club like this one before I came out here. I've done some of this before myself. I'm the guy with the flogger."

"Kim was right—you do know a little about what's going on, don't you?" Kelly smiled.

They turned their attention back to the stage, where the assistant's ankles were now cuffed to a spreader bar. This opened her legs quite wide and suspended her about a foot from the stage floor. The Master turned her slowly to face the wall, then gathered her hair and pulled it over her shoulder, leaving her long, sleek back completely exposed to the audience.

"Now, everyone, please watch my technique," the Master said to the audience. He gave her back several light strokes with the whip from shoulder to shoulder, then moved down to her luscious ass cheeks and continued the whipping. Bryan knew from experience that these light strokes did not cause any pain.

The Master paused occasionally to answer questions from the audience, then continued with the sensuous flogging. After a while, the strokes became harder and the assistant's back turned pink. He stopped, turned her to face the audience, and pulled her hair behind her head, exposing her chest. The

Master started whipping her breasts and nipples, slowly at first, then quickening his pace. Her breasts started to turn red and her nipples seemed to throw the whip back at him after each stroke. She kept her head back so the audience could see the full effect of the whip.

He moved down her body and used an upper cut motion on her pussy lips. This stroke was strong and accurate, and the sound of leather violently hitting skin echoed in the room. "*Ugh!*" she moaned. Each stroke brought another whimper and moan. As the speed and violence of the strokes increased, her moans were louder and her breath became labored. The audience could see the profound pleasure and pain she was enjoying.

The Master seemed to know just when to stop his calculated whipping. After he stopped, the assistant's body continued to jerk and then stiffened as her orgasm washed her over the edge. Sweat was streaming down her face and her cleavage. She let her head fall forward and her hair fell across her chest, covering her breasts.

The Master lowered his assistant to the ground, unfastened her restraints, and wrapped a blanket around her. He smiled down at her and asked the audience, "Any questions?"

Kelly stood up, grabbed Bryan by the hand, and said, "Let's go."

They left the room and continued down the hall toward the deep bass music that was still playing in the distance.

"What are these rooms with the 'Do Not Disturb' signs on them?" Bryan asked.

"A private room for you and your submissive," she told him. "No one but the person in charge of the party can come in. Usually, no one bothers you, and you can do just about anything in there. They don't have as much equipment as the main room, but it's enough."

They moved through a double door into another very large open room, where a large number of people were engaged in just about any type of bondage play you could think of. Kelly started to ease around the room. Bryan followed her, listening to the sounds of leather on skin and deep, grueling moans of ecstasy.

They stopped to watch a woman tied to a spanking bench with her top using a single-tail whip on her ass. The strokes were severe and swift, and red lines marked her ass cheeks and upper back. The submissive's fists were clenched and a noticeable trail of drool had escaped the ball gag in her mouth.

A naked young girl walked by, her hands cuffed behind her, an older man holding her leash. She greeted Kelly as they passed.

"You know her?" Bryan asked.

"For a while now," Kelly answered, looking around the room. "Would you look at that? I'll be damned!" she cried out. "I told you that bastard Ted would get that redheaded bitch in the corner. He's got her strapped to the wall, and look at her back! Maybe it was a good thing I went back upstairs when I did, or that could be me."

As they continued around the room, they saw a naked man trying to walk as a beautiful woman pulled him along by a leather strap tied to his balls, slapping his ass with a riding crop from time to time.

Bryan noticed Bill and Virginia at the other end of the room. Bill had Virginia's arms stretched and her wrists tied to hooks on the wall. There were large nipple clamps attached to Virginia's nipples, and hooked to the clamps were heavy weights.

Kelly noticed his stare. "Bill does that to her all the time. I think they try to see how much weight she can hold."

"Oh, look at Mr. Ling with Amy!" she exclaimed. "My gosh! This is the first time I've seen Japanese rope bondage and suspension in person." Amy was tied in a position like a human ball. "That has to be a strain!" Kelly grabbed Bryan by the hand. "Come on, let's go. I can't take this anymore."

Bryan wasn't really ready to go, but he didn't want to upset anybody. He had seen more than he thought he was going to. "Okay, I'm ready, I guess," he said.

He followed Kelly back into the hall and into one of the small rooms. She hung the "Do Not Disturb" sign on the outside doorknob and closed the door. "Now no one will bother us," she said. The look in her eyes told Bryan that their relationship was about to take a turn in another direction.

Kelly smiled and took off her halter top to expose a pair of strong and demanding breasts. Her incredible nipples were erect and eloquently displayed to Bryan's gaze. A few seconds later, her bottoms were off with her socks and tennis shoes. Bryan removed his clothes, and both of them stood naked, staring at each other.

Bryan took the lead and put his arms around her. She shivered a bit at his strong, manly touch. He pulled her close to his chest, feeling the hardness of her body and the splendor of her nipples and breasts. They looked into each other's eyes and immediately knew their positions.

He forced his tongue into her mouth and kissed her deeply. He played with her submissive tongue, feeling the warmth of her mouth and her inner desire. He knew she was ready to play.

"Come with me now," he said softly, escorting his feline slave to the spanking bench in the middle of the room. She straddled the bench, and he secured her wrists and ankles to its legs. Then Bryan walked around in front of her, grabbed a handful of hair, and pulled her head up to face him. Several seconds passed in silence as he gazed into the sparkle of her dark, sensuous eyes. "You are such a beautiful woman, and I must say, even more so in bondage—a fantasy comes true."

He kissed her again. Her body responded from the depths of her subconscious; her emotions were running high. "I can tell you are a very passionate woman," he said.

He let her head down and moved to stand at her back, lightly touching her rounded ass cheeks, which offered an open view of her ass and pussy. He separated her ass with his fingers, teasing the sensitive folds of her pussy slit.

"I love that, damn, I love that," she moaned. "Please don't stop. Put your finger in and push it to the front, please." But he did stop—he had other things on his mind. His cock, already hard, lay against his lower belly waiting its turn as sweat started to appear on his forehead.

Bryan picked out a riding crop from the wall rack and lightly tapped Kelly's ass. Leather hitting ass cheeks makes a unique sound.

Kelly whimpered from the contact. "*Ugh!*"

He gave her ass another delightful slap and continued until both ass cheeks were quite red and the flame of desire enveloped her body. Then he laid the crop down and selected a smaller whip from the rack display. The braided leather handle was eight inches long with two twelve-inch leather leads—very springy with a lot of sting.

"*Aow*! Damn, that thing stings!" she cried at the first stroke. "Bryan, that really stings." She shifted her ass on the bench and yanked on the wrist cuffs, but they held firm.

"It's just like foreplay for sex, Kelly. A whip is used to stimulate and bring a submissive to slut status." Kelly's back became as red as her ass under his firm, calculated strokes. Her moans and groans grew with each stroke, but Bryan could tell that even though she was sexually excited, she wasn't quite ready to have an orgasm.

He put the whip down and started to stroke his hard cock. Her ass and pussy were just too phenomenal to pass up. "Now, my dear, let's see if this will help you."

With his left hand, he exposed her well-lubricated slit. With his right, he encircled his cock and pushed it in, his belly slapping against her ass cheeks at the initial contact.

"Damn!" she cried, feeling her pussy completely penetrated by his deliciously massive cock, its hardness like a steel rod driving through her body. Streams of fire ravished her body as his pumping action hammered against her sex—slowly at first, then harder. His rhythm was like a machine, each stroke a continuous effort, but no matter what he did, she would not come.

Finally, Bryan reached for his whip, and as he pumped deep into her abyss, he smacked her ass cheeks with a blistering stroke. *Whack*! Then a second stroke. *Whack*!

The sound echoed off the walls of the room. Red welts blossomed on her well-tanned skin.

"Damn! Damn! That's so good! I—I can feel your damned hard cock pulsating inside me, Bryan!" Kelly screamed. Her body stiffened and she held her breath as her pussy released its sweet liquid of love.

He held her until her breathing became more normal, slowing his pumping action, but he knew by the tingle in his balls that his cock was ready to explode. Instead of letting go, he eased his cock from its feminine prison.

"*Aw!*" Kelly felt the shaft leave her. Her stiffened body relaxed on the bench as Bryan walked to her front. He grabbed her hair and pulled her head up to face his raging cock. "Open your mouth!" he ordered. She blinked her submissive eyes and then closed them, obediently opening her mouth to accept his hard shaft.

The combination of the warmth and wetness of her mouth and the strokes he was applying to his cock sent Bryan over the edge: his body stiff, his breath shallow, he came full force in her mouth. Torrents of hot, searing cum shot against the back of her throat, almost causing her to choke from the force of the explosion. "Take it all, but don' swallow it!" His voice quivered a bit as the remaining cum oozed from his cock's purple head.

Bryan eased his cock out of Kelly's mouth, telling her, "Shut your mouth, and do it quickly." She obeyed. A slurping sound escaped her lips. "Now swallow it all! Do it now!" Bryan could see her throat muscles tense as she completed the task he had given her.

She opened her eyes, blinked, and looked at him. "Kelly, use your tongue and clean the head off." His cock was only semi-hard by this time, but she followed his instructions and licked her wet lips with her tongue when she was finished.

He released her from the restraints and they started to dress. "Bryan, you know you and I can never talk about this, right?" Kelly said.

"Don't worry, Kelly," he assured her in his charming way. "My dear beauty, I don't talk out of school."

Together, they left Level Two.

Level Three (Chapter 9)

Bryan arrived at work on Monday as usual, but to his surprise, Kim was not there. Another woman was at the computer, and Kelly was helping her.

"Oh! Morning, Bryan," Kelly said, seeing him come in. "This is Carol. She's gonna be taking Kim's place for a short time. Kim had to fly to New York yesterday—her sister is having an operation, and Kim's taking care of her two kids until she gets back on her feet."

"Nice to meet you, Carol, and welcome to the group." Bryan remembered Carol from the Castaway Club. She seemed a little taller than he remembered, but she'd been sitting behind a counter when he first saw her. She had a very nice body and an amazing schoolgirl face, he thought; it made your mouth water.

"Nice to meet you, Bryan," Carol said with a pixie smile and a little wink nobody saw but him.

Later that morning, Bill called Bryan to his office to meet another potential client. The man was nicely dressed, with a leather briefcase sitting on the floor beside his chair.

"This is Mr. Ted Darling, Bryan," Bill said. "Mr. Darling, Bryan Wescott. Bryan is our International Consultant."

"Nice to meet you, Mr. Darling," Bryan said, shaking the man's hand. It felt like clammy cold steel.

"Mr. Darling, why don't you explain to Bryan where Mr. Rema's interest might be?"

"Well, sir," Darling began, "Mr. Rema has a shipping firm and does a lot of exporting and importing of machinery and repair parts. Over the past two years, he has done exceptionally well, and he wants to invest some of his profits. I'm in charge of security for some of Mr. Rema's bonded warehouses, and he's asked me to represent him in making some quality investments in some American companies.

"Mr. Darling," Bill interrupted, "Bryan will get you our investment package. Please have Mr. Rema review it, sign all the forms, and return it to us, and we'll make the bank transfers for you. Do you have any idea of the amount of money he wishes to invest?"

"Three million," Darling said.

Bryan raised his eyebrows at the figure, but left the office to get the formal investment package from Kelly.

"Mr. Majors," Darling said after Bryan had left the office, "Mr. Rema is a very private person and does not believe in banks. Upon his approval of the documents, I will return with the money in cash."

Bill thought that was a little strange. Handling that kind of money and using no banks? "That's a lot of money to carry around, you know."

"I know, and I agree with you," Darling continued, "but that's the way Mr. Rema wants it. Oh—by the way, you should know me."

"Well, now that you mention it, you do look familiar," said Bill.

"I'm one of the directors of a group that uses the Club for special parties. I also help with volunteers for the Level Three auctions."

Bill studied Darling for a second. He had actually recognized him, but didn't want to let on. "Yes, I do, now that you mention it. We thank you for all your help."

"Mr. Rema is also very interested in having a slot in the auction at the end of this month. Is there some way he can participate?"

Bill reached into his file cabinet, retrieved a thin folder, and handed it to Darling.

"Have Mr. Rema read the rules and regulations, fill out the questionnaire, and return it to George Edwards at the main club—the address is in the folder. George is the director of operations and must approve all applications for the auction. He should turn in the form soon, or he won't get to participate."

"Thank you," Mr. Darling replied, taking the folder and putting it into his briefcase.

Bryan returned with the investment information and presented it to Mr. Darling. "Please feel free to contact me if there are any questions," Bryan said. "My number is in the packet."

"Another client for you, Bryan," Bill said after Darling left the office. "I'm trying to keep you busy."

"You're doing a great job of that," Bryan replied.

"Ask Kelly to step in when you go by her desk," Bill said. He was curious about the way Ted Darling had presented himself.

A few minutes later, Kelly came in.

"Have a seat, Kelly." Bill had a bit of a solemn grimace on his face.

"What's up?" Kelly asked cheerfully. Her mood changed when she saw Bill's expression. "Is there something wrong?"

"Ted Darling was just here. Peggy told me you dated him a few times."

"That's right. I met him at a club one night and we've gone out to eat a few times—nothing serious, though." Kelly looked skeptical. "I saw him leave. What's wrong?"

"He told me he represented a Mr. Tony Rema from Italy and was in charge of security for some bonded warehouses that this guy has. He said Rema has a shipping firm and wants to invest three million dollars cash in some US companies. Sounds a little odd, don't you think?"

Kelly seemed a little perplexed. "I know he's done some security work for some warehouses, but that's all I know. Maybe I should get in touch with my people in Washington—I'm sure they can find out something about this guy Rema. Sounds like this might be a lead worth checking out."

"I'll check with my local people and see if they can come up with anything," Bill said. "I'll let you know."

"You really do think this might be what we've been looking for, don't you?" Kelly asked.

"Well, most normal people don't walk around with three million dollars in cash and avoid banks. He may be trying to launder some illegal money."

"You're right," Kelly said. "I think we may be on to something here."

On the Thursday before the auction, the telephone rang in the front office. "Line two, Bill, it's George Edwards." Peggy put the call through.

"Hi, George, how do things look for Saturday night?" Bill hoped everything was ready. The Club made a major profit from these auctions.

"Things look okay, Bill," George responded. "We have seven bidders who will be at the hotel on Friday. We'll send a car to pick them up on Saturday and bring them to the Club at six. All except a Mr. Tony Rema— Ted Darling, his security guard, will provide his transportation. The bidders include a mistress from California, two men from Chicago, a man from Las Vegas, a man from England named 'Lord Baltic,' Mr. Ling, and Mr. Rema. Ted Darling has informed me he has four women volunteers, with a fifth one who's out of town but may be back in time for the auction. He's not real sure on that."

"If four is all we got, I guess we'll have to go with that," said Bill. "Let me know if there are any changes."

On Saturday afternoon, Bryan had just settled down to watch a game on TV when there came a knock on his door.

"Kelly! Come on in." He gestured with his hand. "Would you like a beer or a spanking?"

"No thanks—not tonight, maybe later. But I do need your help, that is, if you're interested?" Kelly stood at the door, her arms folded.

"Sure thing! If I can be of some help to you, by all means."

"Would you be an observer with me tonight at the Level Three auction?" she asked. "I think you might enjoy the event."

"I'd love to," he said.

Bryan thought he knew what would happen, but he wasn't sure.

They left his apartment and went to the Club, stopping at Level One for a drink. Peggy was the only one on duty at the bar, dressed in Bryan's favorite outfit.

"Kelly," Peggy said, "I just found out that the fifth woman came back in time for tonight. It's who we expected." She did not use any names.

Kelly shook her head, but said nothing. After their drink, Kelly took Bryan down the back steps to Level Two. They walked down to the end of the hall and got into an elevator. After a very short ride down, the doors opened to reveal a sign on the wall that read "Level Three." They continued down a small hallway to the right that reminded Bryan of a hotel. There were five doors on his left, numbered one through five. Opposite room number four, on the right, was a door marked "Observers." Kelly opened this door and showed him in.

The observers' room was small, but big enough for a table and a few chairs. A tray of drinks and mixers sat in the middle of the table, and Kelly fixed a drink for each of them. "Take your drink and follow me," she said, opening another door and stepping out onto a small glassed-in balcony that overlooked a much larger room.

Kelly gestured for Bryan to sit down beside her in the plush high-backed leather loveseat on the balcony. "No one can see in, but we can see out," she whispered.

Below them, Bryan could see a podium and seven numbered chairs in a row behind a pedestal. Above the pedestal, a cable with an "O" ring at the end hung from a pulley in the ceiling. Five human-sized metal cages stood along the wall of the large room.

"Bryan," Kelly whispered, "I know you want to know what's happening, so settle back and listen up." He adjusted himself in his seat, and Kelly continued. "This afternoon, five women volunteers were picked up at the Castaway Club and driven here. They're behind that door next to the cages, in a small holding room. Each woman is totally nude except for leather cuffs on her wrists and ankles, a leather collar locked around her neck, and a ball gag in her mouth buckled around her head. They will remain like this until midnight."

A man and a woman came in through the holding room door. "Here come Warren and Beth," Kelly said.

The woman sat down at a small desk and opened a laptop computer. "Warren is the auctioneer, and Beth is his secretary. She'll do all the paperwork." Kelly paused, then continued, "There are seven bidders. They will enter from the door to our left and sit in the numbered chairs. Okay, here they come now."

Each bidder leisurely walked in and took a seat.

"No one will talk to us, and we won't talk to anyone," Kelly said. "We are to observe and report on anything that may be asked of us; all parties know we're here. It's a safety issue."

"Good evening, ladies and gentlemen," Warren said as he took his position behind the podium. "I would like to welcome you seven bidders to our most unusual auction." He gestured to his right as another man entered the room.

"This is Mr. George Edwards, the head of operations here at the Club. What he says is final."

Edwards acknowledged the bidders and sat down in a lounge chair on one side of the room.

"All of you have completed the proper forms to be at this auction," said Warren.

"As you saw coming in, there are six security officers at the entrance door. They will not bother you in any of your endeavors tonight, but if they are required to assist the Club with security, I can assure you they will.

"Please be informed that above you are two concealed observers. They will monitor your activities tonight for safety reasons, but will not interfere in any way." Kelly pressed a button and a green light came on. "As you can see, they are present."

Warren continued with his instructions. "If our volunteers suffer any serious injury, you will be fully responsible for their recovery and health care. When you win a bid, your personal bags will be immediately taken to your assigned room. Now, please register with Beth and present the proper fee, one at a time, beginning with Number One."

The first bidder walked up to Beth and opened a briefcase full of cash. "Twenty-five thousand," Kelly whispered to Bryan.

Beth typed something on her laptop, took the money, and placed it in a box. After every bidder had paid, she nodded to Warren.

"Now that that's over, let's have the first lady!" Warren announced. He pressed a button, and the door beside the cages opened.

Bryan almost fell out of his seat when he saw Pat Howard come through the door. She was as stunning as ever, dressed in a black patent leather jumpsuit that glistened in the dim light. A large bullwhip was attached to a belt around her narrow waist, and she was leading Bill's friend Virginia by a leather and chain leash.

Pat positioned Virginia on the pedestal, attached her cuffed wrists to the "O" ring, and turned the crank on the hoist to stretch her body until her feet just barely touched the floor.

"Bidders, you may now walk around and view the first lady for bid,"

Warren said. "Please remember, do not touch."

Several of the bidders commented on Virginia's figure, and one asked whether she could take several hours of restraint. They all agreed she could. When the bidders returned to their seats, Pat took her down, cuffed her hands behind her back, and put her in the first cage.

The second lady to enter with Pat was Alice. Bryan's eyes opened wide again when he recognized her. The last time he saw her, she'd been suspended at the Castaway Club with Mack whipping her. She was a gorgeous woman with a figure to match any he'd ever seen. The same procedure applied to Alice as to Virginia: her wrists were cuffed to the cable and her body stretched, the bidders observed her, and then Pat led her to the next cage.

The third lady was Carol, and the fourth was Bryan's beloved Kim. Bryan almost choked on his drink when he saw her.

"Be quiet, Bryan!" Kelly whispered. "Peggy and I thought she would be the one. You have to know, Kim is extremely submissive and goes much further than most of us. She told me once that it's a need deep inside her to be totally helpless and lose control. The emotion overwhelms her. She craves being a slave, accepts the pain, and relishes the pleasure. She needs to serve a man's needs, regardless of what he wants."

Pat smiled at Kim and took extra time securing her leather cuffs to the cable. As she stepped away from the pedestal, she lightly patted Kim's bottom. It was obvious to Bryan that she wanted Kim.

Pat went to the hoist to pull Kim's body taut; this time, however, she cranked it far enough that Kim's feet left the floor for a second or two. Bryan knew she had done it on purpose just to look at Kim's suspended body. He had to admit that Kim was an amazing woman who made the racing chart with her figure.

The fifth and final lady to come through the door was Amy. Bryan saw Mr. Ling move to the edge of his seat, and his mind raced back to the time when Mr. Ling had done some interesting things to Amy on Level Two. From what Bryan could remember, Amy had enjoyed herself as much as Mr. Ling had, but this was a new ball game.

Pat displayed Amy like the others, then locked her into cage number five. The bidders had ten minutes to walk around and view the cages.

After the time was up, Warren announced, "Ladies and gentlemen, please take your seats and we will start the bidding. Pat, if you please, bring out number one again."

Pat led Virginia back to the pedestal and posed her facing the bidders.

"The bidding will start at five thousand," Warren said. Several minutes later, the woman from California won with a bid of fifteen thousand dollars. After she paid, Pat handed her Virginia's leash.

"Congratulations on your bid and your prize," Warren said. "A tone will sound in your room at 11:45; at that time, you will need to escort your lady back to this room. Pat will inspect her, and if she approves, you may leave."

The woman nodded and walked out of the room, leading her new sex slave.

Alice was next, and one of the men from Chicago won her for twenty thousand.

"Sir, congratulations on your bid. Your ending time will be 11:48, and at that time, Pat will make her inspection."

Alice's new master led her away, and Carol was next on the block. Bryan took a good look at her from his position in the observation area. She was a little taller than Alice and her breasts were a little smaller, but he could tell her nipples were bigger.

"Gentlemen, as you can see, things are thinning out a bit. The starting bid is five thousand." Everyone put a bid in for Carol, but the man from Vegas won with eighteen thousand. "Sir, your time is 11:50," Warren informed the bidder. He paid his fee and took Carol's leash.

Kim came out next. Pat stroked her bottom again as she stepped onto the pedestal and stared out at the remaining bidders. Before Warren could start the bidding process, Tony Rema put his hand up. "Fifteen thousand!"

Lord Baltic from England chimed in, "Twenty thousand!"

"Twenty-one!" said the other man from Chicago.

"*Twenty-five!*" Rema yelled like a man possessed, glaring around at the others. He won the bid. After paying his fee, he took his captive and left the room.

Amy was next and seemed a little apprehensive to step on the pedestal. Pat yanked on her leash, and Bryan could see that it got the message across; she stepped up. The three remaining men bid furiously, but Mr. Ling finally put the icing on the cake with a twenty-two-thousand-dollar bid.

"Congratulations, sir, you may take your slave. Your time is 11:58," Warren informed Mr. Ling. Mr. Ling took the leash and Amy followed with a small smile on her face.

"For the two gentlemen that did not win a bid," Warren said, "if you will see Beth, she will return one half of your registration fee. Complimentary dinner and drinks are ready for you in the main bar upstairs."

As the remaining bidders left the room, George Edwards stood up. "Warren that was a very good job. I'll be in my office if there are any problems. I should be back by 11:30."

"Yes, sir," Warren replied. "Beth and I will tally the totals, make out the envelopes for the women, and have everything ready." George nodded and left the room.

"Let's go, Bryan," Kelly said. "All of the guests should be in their rooms now and starting their sessions. We'll take a walk around and observe what they're doing." She fixed him another drink, then led him to another hallway on the far side of the building where large double-paned windows offered a complete view of each private room.

"They can't hear or see us," Kelly said, "but we can see everything they're doing."

There was a bench against the opposite wall, so they sat down to watch the lady from California with Virginia. She had changed into a black leather halter top that revealed most of her abundant chest and a miniskirt that would have barely covered her panties if she were wearing any; black stiletto heels finished off the outfit.

"Bryan," Kelly said, "you wondered why there was so much money on the table for this auction. Well, there are no limits to what these people can do to their slaves; there are no safe words or stopping points. These people are savage about what they're doing, and they're all well practiced in the art of sadism. They enjoy inflicting as much pain and torment as their slave can handle without major injuries."

Virginia was hanging by her wrist cuffs from a cable in the ceiling, her legs chained together with her feet about two feet off the floor. Her mistress took a smooth, catlike approach, taking her time to study her sensual prey. Then she brought out a whip. The whip was short with many tails, and it cut Virginia's ass with a fury only Virginia could tell.

Bryan knew from his own experience that the strokes were severe and very painful. He watched her entire body jerk with each stroke. Her teeth showed over he ball gag as drool escaped from the corners her mouth.

Stroke after stroke covered her body, in front and in back. Finally, Virginia's head dropped, her hair fell between her cleavage, and she passed out.

"Next," Kelly said, grabbing Bryan by the hand and pulling him away. They moved down the hall to observe Alice in the next room.

Alice was hanging upside down with her wrists bound to eyehole hooks on the wall and her feet spread apart by a spreader bar. Clothespins were attached to her pussy lips with a wire around each thigh to pull the lips apart. The wires, just barely visible, cut deep into her skin, and Bryan could see directly into her vagina.

The bidder from Chicago was naked with one hand on his cock and a two-leather popper whip in the other hand. He walked around her, stroking his cock as he watched her try to handle the pain. When the popper whip found its mark against Alice's sex, her entire body shivered and her head jerked from side to side trying to fight it.

"She's not going anywhere for a while. Let's check on Carol," Kelly said.

Bryan was fascinated by the abuse Alice's pussy was receiving, but he followed Kelly's lead.

In the next room, Carol was lying on a long table with her wrists and ankles secured to the front and back legs of the table. Her nipples were rock-hard, jutting upwards from her breasts, which stood up like two little hills. Her pubic hair was short and manicured, just like a green on a golf course.

The guy from Vegas was stroking his large cock while he moved between her legs, but seemed to have no intention of penetration. He stopped masturbating long enough to pick up a razor, then applied some cream to Carol's pussy and started to shave her pubic hair.

"Can he do that, Kelly?" Bryan gestured to the man.

"Oh, yes, he sure can," Kelly replied. "He can't cut her head hair, but the pussy hair can go. I'm surprised he used cream, and I wonder if that razor has a sharp blade in it."

They continued to watch as he finished the shave and lit a candle, then slowly dripped hot red wax over Carol's pubic mound and into her crevice. Bryan and Kelly could see her body shake as she tried to scream. Her teeth bit down on the ball gag and her eyes burned with fury at the pain of the hot wax. He continued to wax her pussy like a ceremonial ritual, each drop of wax placed in just the right spot.

In the fourth room, Mr. Rema was completely nude and stroking his cock like the others. Kim was suspended about three feet off the floor with her body stretched as far as it would go; her cuffed wrists and ankles secured spreader bars. Her hair was tied with a thin rope and attached to the ceiling cable, pulling her head up.

Rema held a braided black leather whip, about four feet long, with an eight-inch handle. It separated halfway down into two more lengths of braided leather, and at the end of the whip were four poppers that could deliver very nasty cuts. He tested the whip in midair a couple of times, then delivered the first cut to Kim's right breast and nipple. Her breast bounced at the whip's contact, and red lines appeared on her skin. Her hands became fists, she shut her eyes, and her body shook. Drool oozed from behind her ball gag. In minutes, Kim's entire chest was a mass of red welts.

"Enough of this, Bryan, we have one more to see," Kelly said. She knew that Rema was a real bastard, and she also knew that Bryan had some deep feelings for Kim. She grabbed Bryan's hand and had to jerk him to make him follow her down the hall a few steps to the last room.

Kelly did a double-take when she saw Amy tied and suspended from the ceiling in a ball of nude flesh, her ass and pussy wide open for view and whipping as Mr. Ling adjusted her Japanese rope bondage.

"The Japanese have a way with rope, don't they?" Kelly remarked.

Bryan noticed a vibrator deep in Amy's pussy; only a small portion was visible. That brought back memories of Sally at Nick's house, and he wondered how they were doing.

Mr. Ling picked up a riding crop and started applying red marks to Amy's body. Her body swayed after each hit, and Mr. Ling had to stop her swing so he could hit her again.

Kelly and Bryan walked back down the hall, and as they passed each room, looked in to see what else was happening. Whips fell in a few different positions, but nothing much had changed. They could tell the constant torment the women were enduring was taking its toll.

"Okay, Bryan, it's time we got back to the balcony," Kelly said. "The ending time is getting close." Minutes later, they were sitting on their leather couch looking down into the bidding room, drinks in hand. Mr. Edwards was in his seat; Warren and Beth were in theirs. Pat walked out from the room behind the cages and joined the others.

The first tone sounded, and in walked the lady from California with Virginia in tow. She handed Pat the leash.

"Are you all right, my dear?" Pat asked. Her gag was still in place, but Virginia nodded. Pat looked at Warren and gave an okay sign.

"Thank you," Warren said to the California lady. "If you will wait in the conference room upstairs, your ride to the hotel will be taken care of shortly." She walked out as Pat escorted Virginia to the back room.

Alice came in next, red marks still showing on her body. Her hair was disheveled and she walked very slowly. Carol followed; the guy from Vegas had removed most of the wax from her body, but traces were still visible. Pat took both women's leashes and led them to the back room.

Mr. Rema took his sweet time returning to the bidding room. They were about to send for him when he entered with Kim in tow. Her walk seemed pathetic and slow; she could barely take a step without help. It was not difficult to see that the session had taken a lot out of her.

Pat examined the welts on Kim's body, then glared at Rema. If looks could kill, Rema would have taken his last breath. She turned back to Kim. "Are you all right, my dear?" Kim raised her head and stared at Pat, but did not answer.

"Are you *all right*, my dear?" Pat repeated, a little louder.

Rema put a hand under Kim's chin, lifted her head, and glared at her with his cold steely eyes. "Tell her you're all right!" He dropped his hand, and Kim's head dropped.

Pat turned her head away like a cat ready to strike at another animal stealing its only meal. She repeated her question. "*Are you sure?*" Pat was about ready to take a whip to Rema.

Finally, Kim nodded to indicate that she was okay, and Rema turned and left the room. Pat did not take the leash this time, but put her arm around Kim's waist and walked her to the back room.

Amy came in last with Mr. Ling, who had an incredible smile on his face. "Me thank you for session. Me had great time with young lady. Like do again." Mr. Ling gave the leash to Pat, and Amy affirmed that she was fine. Pat led Amy to the back room with the others, followed her in, and closed the door.

"What's the tally, Warren?" George Edwards asked, standing up.

Warren looked to Beth for the report. Beth opened her computer and read, "The Club made $137,500. Our first lady tallied $20,000. Our second lady tallied $22,500. Our third lady tallied $21,500. The fourth lady was high with $25,000. The fifth lady was second with $23,500." Warren looked at Mr. Edwards and smiled.

"That's a very good night. Very good work from the both of you," Edwards said.

"Take care of Pat with the usual and deposit the rest. Again, thank you for a great job." He looked up at the observer station and said in a louder voice, "Very good job, and thank you, observers."

Kelly cut the green light off as Mr. Edwards left the room. "I'm going to check on Kim and the other girls," she said to Bryan. "I think you can find your way out?"

Bryan looked at Kelly with a worried expression. "Do you think Kim is okay? She had a very hard time with Rema."

Kelly was concerned, but tried not to show it. "Yep, she's okay. I just want to be sure, that's all."

Bryan made his way back upstairs to the bar, where Peggy was just closing up. "Well, Bryan, things are closed for the night," she said. "Would you walk me to my car?"

"I'd love to," he said.

In the parking lot, Peggy found her car. Just before she got in, she asked Bryan, "How did you like Level Three and the auction?"

"Amazing, just amazing," he said.

"Bryan, you are a really nice guy. I know you like to play, and a lot of us do. We're not a bad lot, you know." She touched his cheek, then moved closer and Bryan felt her soft, sensuous lips touch his—no tongue action, just a loving kiss. Then she turned, got into her car, and drove off.

The Ring Harness (Chapter 10)

Early Sunday afternoon, Bryan fired up his small grill. He liked grilling steak; there was just something about the smell of the meat and the charcoal.

It wasn't long before Mr. Ling walked up and sat down in the patio chair. "Me love smell, Miser Bryan," he said.

"Me too, Mr. Ling. Want a steak and a beer?"

"You bet," said the Japanese man, smiling and taking a chair. During dinner, Bryan went over the results of his work on the reformat of the investments for Mr. Ling and his fellow investors.

The telephone rang, and Bryan answered the call. "Bryan, it's Pat Howard. Do you have the item we discussed? I have Alice with me, and I would like to stop by and get it."

"Yes, I do, and please come by. I do need her to adjust the fittings."

"See you in about thirty minutes," Pat said and hung up.

"Business call?" Mr. Ling asked.

"Yep, it sure was," he replied, sitting back down with his beer.

"Me need leave then?"

"No, no," Bryan said. "I think you might like to be involved with this, Mr. Ling."

"As you wish, Miser Bryan."

Their dinner finished, they had moved to the living room to discuss the investments when the doorbell rang. Bryan opened the door. Pat was standing there looking as lovely as ever in a very revealing pair of shorts and top, and beside her was Alice in a similar outfit. The only difference was that Alice had a very large black leather collar around her neck and Pat was holding a chain and leather leash attached to her collar.

"Come in, ladies." Bryan stepped back to let them enter the room. "Have a seat. And would you guys like a beer?"

"Yes, I would," Pat responded, "but Alice can't right now." Pat sat in the lounge chair across from Mr. Ling, and Alice knelt down at her feet.

Bryan returned from the kitchen with beers for everyone except Alice. "Pat Howard, this is Mr. Ling. Mr. Ling, Pat Howard. Both of you are clients of mine."

"Nice meet you, Miss Howard." Mr. Ling bowed his head.

Pat returned the greeting. "It's nice to meet you, too, Mr. Ling," she said, "but didn't I see you last night at the Club?"

"Ah, yes. Me there. Me come to US to invest money with Miser Majors; he take me to Club and Level Three."

Pat felt a little better about Mr. Ling. She only hoped Bryan knew what he was doing, having Mr. Ling at his house during their meeting.

"Mr. Ling, this is Alice," Bryan said. "She's Pat's property, but Pat has had some difficulty with her. She's asked me to help promote her training."

Mr. Ling looked down at the beautiful young woman sitting on the floor with her arms behind her back. "Nice meet you, Alice."

Alice glanced at Pat, who nodded. Alice then looked back to Mr. Ling. Her voice was soft and meek. "Nice to meet you, sir."

"Okay, Bryan, let's see what you've got," said Pat.

Bryan went to the hall closet, brought back a large paper bag, and pulled out a large leather harness with a lot of "O" rings attached.

Pat was surprised at the amount of leather involved. "How does it work?"

"Mr. Ling, would you get a low-back chair from the dining room?"

"Sure Miser Bryan." A few seconds later, Mr. Ling placed the chair in the middle

of the living room facing the couch.

"Okay, Alice, would you please sit down in the chair?" Bryan asked.

"Not yet, Bryan," Pat said. "Alice, up!" Alice immediately stood up. "Remove your clothes, Alice, all of them."

Bryan and Mr. Ling watched Alice disrobe. She was a vision of loveliness. There was no sag in Alice's breasts; they were a little larger than some, but soft and firm. Her nipples were rigid and standing erect. Bryan quickly noticed that she sported no pussy hair, providing a very open view of her slit. He smiled inwardly and wondered who had done the shaving.

When Alice was naked, Pat said, "You may sit down in the chair now," then moved to the couch so she could face Alice.

"Alice," Bryan instructed, "please put your hands behind your back, palms together." Alice immediately complied. Bryan looped a small rope around her wrists and cinched them together. With a second rope, he tied her elbows together, thrusting her breasts forward; her nipples were rock-hard by this time. The next piece of rope secured her wrists and elbows to the chair back.

"Spread your legs, Alice, one on each side of the chair seat," Bryan ordered. Slowly, she moved her legs to the sides of the chair. He took another rope and wrapped it around her right ankle.

"Bend your leg at the knee," Pat commanded. Bryan tied the rope to the back leg of the chair, pulling Alice's right leg backwards, then did the same with her left leg.

"Pat, watch now as I put this on her. The adjustments are very fine and need to be just right." He pulled the harness over the top of Alice's head. Bryan was only inches from Alice's face, and he could smell her womanly odor; it was intoxicating, deepening his desire to see her enveloped in the harness. As he looked deep into her beautiful dark eyes, he could see them sparkle with concern about her fate. It had an unfathomable effect on him and his third leg. "Alice," he said softly, "this will not hurt you. It will be tight, but you shouldn't feel any pain." His comment seemed to reassure her, and the strained look in her face softened.

Bryan placed a large round metal ring on the top of her head. A leather strap with a buckle attached to the ring went down the back of her head, and he secured it loosely to her leather collar. Two straps with small "O" rings, also attached to the head ring, lay against the sides of her face. Another leather strap buckled around her head with leather patches that covered her eyes, taking away her sight.

The next strap held the "O" ring for her mouth. "Alice, I want you to swallow and then open your mouth as wide as you can." She obeyed, and Bryan inserted the ring behind her lower and upper front teeth. "Let your mouth relax now." As she did, Bryan tightly buckled the strap behind her head.

A chinstrap buckled to the rings on her cheeks held everything in place. Two more straps attached to the ring on her head came down over her eyes and buckled to the chinstrap. Bryan then returned to the first strap behind her head and tightened it to make sure her mouth was open and her head held in place.

He stood back. "Okay, Pat, please inspect the harness."

"My word," she said, "that is one of the most exquisite harnesses I've ever seen. Is the ring in her mouth big enough for a man's cock?"

"Of course it is." Bryan didn't tell her that he'd measured the ring to fit his own cock. As Pat walked around Alice inspecting the harness, Bryan pointed out that if she were in her dungeon, Alice's head could be tied on each side to eyebolts on the wall. She could tie the head ring to a beam above her to hold her head up, or position her head against a beam and secure it there; either way, she wouldn't be able to move. "Well, what do you think?" Bryan asked, he was proud of his invention.

"Fantastic job, and very professional, I might add. I can only see one thing missing in this little demonstration of yours," Pat said.

"What might that be?" he replied.

"Does it work? Her mouth is open and her head is encased in your harness, but you know my problem with her. Does this thing work?"

"Pat, I have seen this work every time. It works, I can assure you of that."

"Show me, then. I want to see if it really does work."

"You mean you want me to come in her mouth?" Bryan asked.

"That's right," Pat said, smiling. "Let's see what you've got."

Bryan looked at Pat for a few seconds and didn't say anything. Then he glanced at Mr. Ling, who was thoroughly intrigued by the proceedings. "Me think you need show her, Miser Bryan," Ling said.

Slowly, Bryan began to take off his clothes until he stood buck naked in front of Mr. Ling and Pat, who smiled at the sight of his majestic erection. "Not bad—not bad at all. It's a little larger than I expected. It's really nice, Bryan," she said approvingly.

The veins in his cock protruded from its shaft as he stroked it, the purple head bobbing to each stroke. Being so close to Alice had already turned him on, and now this! He put one leg on each side of the chair; his cock now only inches from Alice's mouth. He touched her legs, and her body heat seemed to increase at his touch. At this rate, he could come before he even touched her mouth with his cock. The sight of this lovely woman completely helpless before him was unbelievable.

Pat could see how excited he was. "Hold on there, buddy, not yet," she said. "I want her to come first." With that, she went to one knee on Alice's right side, put a hand between her legs, and started to massage her already wet pussy.

Bryan could feel Alice move to accept the penetration of Pat's finger. "*Ah!*" she moaned from behind the gag. Pat's finger was completely lost from view in her pussy, and she continued to masturbate her. Soon, nature took its course and Alice's body started to stiffen; Bryan could feel her body heat increase even more, signaling that she was close to orgasm. Beads of sweat appeared on her chest and ran down her cleavage.

He cupped her left breast and massaged the flesh, then pinched her nipple, and her body shook at the touch. He held her right breast in the same way and pinched a little harder; again, she shook from the contact.

Then Bryan slid his cock inside her mouth and made contact with her tongue. The combination of having her pussy masturbated, completely helpless, and her mouth wide open with a cock touching her tongue sent Alice over the edge: she came and came and came. Her prominently displayed orgasm was awesome. Pat eased her finger out of Alice's pussy and pulled her arm back, brushing her arm against Bryan's upper thigh and touching his cock. Her skin was soft as she moved away.

Bryan pushed his cock further into Alice's mouth. The heat from her breathing was like an oven. Her tongue traced and massaged the underside of his cock while her head bobbed up and down against his shaft. Bryan put his left hand behind her head to steady it.

Only a short time passed before Bryan could feel his release was near. He pressed his cock against Alice's tongue and started humping her mouth as if it were her pussy. "*Ah! Ah!*" Bryan's body stiffened and his cum shot deep against her throat like a water balloon exploding after hitting a wall. Sweat ran down his face and chest. He continued to pump her face while more cum oozed from the purple head of his swollen cock.

Finished, he looked at Pat and nodded. She picked up the two-pronged whip from the coffee table and stepped to Alice's right side. Bryan eased his cock out of Alice's mouth, and then Pat swung the whip and hit the unsuspecting Alice on her right ass cheek. Her body jerked at the searing pain. A second stroke, and red marks instantly appeared.

Bryan had recovered enough breath to talk by this time. "Look at her throat muscles, Pat, see how they are beating? She's swallowing the cum. She can't scream. She can only suck in air to handle the sting of the whip. When she sucks in air, she can't help but swallow the cum."

"Well, I'll be damned! It does work," Pat said. "That's incredible."

"Every time." Bryan moved away from Alice and sat down on the couch.

Pat inspected the harness, tugging on some of the straps. "Are you sure it works every time?"

"Absolutely," Bryan replied. He nodded to Mr. Ling. "Mr. Ling, would you like to have a go?"

Mr. Ling looked like he had just won the lottery. "You bet, me like have go at Miss Alice!"

He stood up, undressed, and moved into the position that Bryan had just vacated. Mr. Ling's cock wasn't as large as Bryan's, but he wasn't embarrassed by it. With his right hand, he stroked his cock until it was at full erection, then entered Alice's mouth.

"Put your hand behind her head," Bryan said. "It will keep her still."

Mr. Ling followed Bryan's advice and held Alice's head with his left hand. With the other, he cupped and squeezed her left breast, then pinched the nipple, making Alice jump in the chair. He moved his hand to her right breast, then pushed his cock further into her mouth, thrusting until Alice's nose bumped against his stomach. Mr. Ling took a deep breath. "*Ugh! Ugh!*" His cum shot deep into her throat, and he continued his pumping action until his cock was almost soft.

Pat picked up the whip and moved to Alice's left side. As Mr. Ling eased his cock from her mouth, Pat swung the whip and made solid contact with Alice's left ass cheek.

Alice stiffened, but did not swallow. A second stroke, stronger than the first, produced the same effect.

Pat looked at Bryan, who was watching intently. He gestured for her to wait a few seconds, then nodded, and she swung the whip again. When the third stroke cracked across Alice's side, Alice sucked in air and swallowed. She had not expected another strike.

"Look at her throat muscles, Pat," Bryan said, pointing to Alice. "She's taking it all down."

"That was a little different," Pat responded.

"Well, it's a game now," he informed her. "She knows you will whip her, and she will try to anticipate the strike. She will have to breathe at some point. You need to use the whip when she's ready. It really does work every time."

Mr. Ling returned to the couch, totally drained.

"Did you enjoy yourself, Mr. Ling?" Bryan asked.

"Me like coming in US. Never know what expect."

While inspecting the ring harness, Pat noticed the sweat on Alice's face and between her breasts. For Alice to sweat, Pat knew, her sexuality had to be taken to the limit. She was very pleased.

Bryan went to the kitchen and returned with another round of beers for everyone, including Alice. "Okay, Pat, you can release her now."

Pat removed all the rope restraints except the ring harness. Alice slowly moved her arms and legs and sat up a bit in the chair.

"Alice," Bryan said, "Pat is going to remove the harness, but listen to my instructions. The three of us have the same whips that have just been used on you. The directions I'll give you aren't hard to follow, but if you don't do it, you'll be restrained just as before and all of us will see how much whipping you can take. Do you understand?"

Alice nodded.

"Pat, unbuckle the head strap attached to her collar." Bryan waited until the buckle was loose. "Loosen the eye strap. Good, that's fine. Now the mouth ring strap, unbuckle that—now the chin strap. Okay, Alice, Pat is going to slip the ring out of your mouth. When she does, slowly close your mouth."

When the ring slid out of her mouth, Alice closed her mouth. Pat eased the harness off her face and head, and Alice's eyes opened for the first time in almost two hours. She blinked.

"It will take a few minutes for you to get your sight back," Bryan said. "Just let it happen. Now, I have a beer in front of me, and I want you to take as much in your mouth as you can, but do not swallow it until I tell you to."

Alice took the beer and took as much in her mouth as she could hold. Bryan waited a few seconds. "Now swallow it." She did.

"What was that for?"

"Well, Pat, it's like this—if there was any cum left in her mouth, it's certainly been swallowed now, don't you think?"

Pat sat down and just looked at Bryan and Mr. Ling, both men still in the nude. "I must admit, you were right, it works every time. I'll be trying it again soon."

"That's why I showed you the adjustments. I know it will get a lot of use."

"Okay, Alice, get dressed, we have to go." Pat reached into her pocket and pulled out a check for three hundred dollars.

"Wow, that's a lot of money," Bryan said. "I didn't expect that."

"Well, it was worth every cent of it. You know, if you make a couple more of these, I think I can sell them at the club."

"I'll see what I can do."

Pat attached the leash to Alice's collar and said, "Let's go, dear, I'm starving." She pulled on the collar, and Alice followed her to the door.

"I'm hungry too, Mistress Pat," Alice said.

"My dear Alice, you have already had your supper. I'm the one who needs something to eat." She pulled on the collar again.

Bryan opened the door and Pat stepped out onto the small porch. Alice quickly turned her head to look at Bryan, smiled, and winked at him. He returned the look and nodded as if to say, "You're welcome."

Bryan and Mr. Ling stood at the door and watched through the car windshield as Alice sat down in the passenger car seat. Pat produced a pair of handcuffs and cuffed Alice's hands in front of her. She attached the cuffs to a small chain in the floor.

She took a rope and wrapped it around the seat and Alice, securing her to the car seat, then placed a small blanket over her lap to cover her bondage and fastened the seat belt. Pat waved to Bryan and Mr. Ling and drove off.

"Me need go home now, Miser Bryan," said Mr. Ling. "Long flight tomorrow. Miss Kelly pick me up early in morning."

"Okay, Mr. Ling, I'll see you in a few weeks." Bryan lay down on the couch and fell asleep.

The Reversal (Chapter 11)

Bryan was surprised that no one said a word about the Level Three auction during the following week. He realized that the people around him were as

serious about BDSM as he was—including the submissive women, which surprised him even more.

He had just left Bill's office, where they had discussed Ted Darling and the news that Mr. Rema would be investing three million dollars in cash. Bill didn't think the money would actually show up, but Bryan still had to produce a package for the man.

As Bryan walked by the front desk, he glanced over at Kim, Kelly, and Peggy. *My, my*, he thought. *I feel like I've gone to heaven. These three women are a fantasy come true.* He shook his head and continued to his office.

The fax machine clicked to life with a message. Peggy watched it print two pages, then pulled the paper from the paper tray. This fax machine appeared to be an ordinary office machine, but it only sent and received special encrypted messages.

Peggy scanned the papers, then pulled Kelly into Bill's office and shut the door. Kim sat there stunned, wondering what the hell was going on.

"What's up?" Bill asked, a little flabbergasted at their entrance.

"We just got a fax from the main office in Washington," Peggy replied.

"British intelligence just contacted our people. It seems that three days ago, several undercover agents attacked a band of extremists somewhere in the Afghan mountains. They captured one of their lieutenants and made him talk—I really don't want to know how they did that. Anyway, he told them that about two months ago, military trucks delivered a large supply of weapons and ammunition to their group. Several of the crates were marked 'Tony Rema Shipping.' He also told them that a man from the trucks brought two very attractive white women into his leader's tent. The women were naked, gagged, handcuffed, and leashed. He said his leader gave this big Italian a lot of American dollars for the guns, the ammo, and the two women."

"British intelligence said that this Tony Rema has been under investigation for a long time, but they haven't been able to prove that he's running guns or white slaves. Every ship of Rema's has been inspected and nothing has been out of place. This is the first bit of real evidence that this guy is dirty—very dirty."

"Our guy Darling could be up to his eyeballs in this thing," said Bill. "This is a lot bigger than we expected." He looked at Kelly. "Darling's investing a large sum of money for Rema. Would it be right to assume that Rema's using us to launder that money?"

"I think so," Kelly said. "We also know that Darling is involved with a couple of groups that enjoy the BDSM lifestyle. We know he is a prime helper for volunteers for the Level Three auctions. Most importantly, though, we know he does security work in some bonded warehouses that belong to Rema, and we know he got him in last week's auction. It sounds like he's very much involved."

Okay, then," Bill agreed, "I'll get my locals to do a little investigating into some of his activities, and if something turns up, I'll let you two know."

The week was finally over, and all Bryan wanted to do was get home, take a shower, grab a beer, and just relax. He had just flopped down on his couch and turned the TV on when he heard a knock on the door. To his surprise, it was Peggy, still dressed in her office attire.

"Come on in," he said, waving her in. "What have I done to deserve the honor of your visit?"

Peggy stepped into the living room. "Kim and Kelly are working at the Club tonight. I've got to work again tomorrow night, so this is the only night I get to go out to eat. Would you like to join me for some Italian? I know a scrumptious little place near Pikes Point."

Bryan hadn't even thought about food, but Peggy was a ravishing young woman, and he loved to spend time with beautiful women. He remembered the surprising kiss she had given him in the parking lot. "I do love Italian, and now that you mention it, I'm starving. Why not?"

"Great! I'll drive," she said.

Bryan recognized their surroundings as they approached Pikes Point and commented that he had looked at a house in the area. "Margaret Lewis from Lewis Real Estate showed it to me," he told Peggy.

"I know that place," Peggy remarked. "I looked at it about a year ago myself. It's out of my price range, though. The husband died and the wife's health was bad, so she moved back north someplace—at least that's what I was told."

Bryan shook his head. "Margaret told me the same thing about the husband and wife. It's a nice place; they took very good care of it."

A few minutes later, Peggy stopped the car in front of a place called Rosa's, where they enjoyed a fabulous meal with a very expensive bottle of Chardonnay. As always, Bryan, the gentleman, picked up the tab.

When they returned to the car, a diminutive evil smirk appeared on Peggy's schoolgirl face. "Would you like something a little stronger than that wine?"

"You bet," Bryan replied. "I've always been told, never turn down an offer like that from a exquisite lady."

Peggy took him back to her house. When they entered, she immediately dropped her pocketbook on the couch and headed down the hall, shouting back to Bryan, "Fix us a couple of drinks from the bar! I'm gonna change into something more comfortable."

Bryan mixed the drinks, then called to her, "I've got your drink ready! Are you?"

"Bring it down the hall, Bryan!"

He quietly made his way down to her open bedroom door and peeked in. Peggy was naked except for a glossy black G-string, standing in front of the mirror and putting her hair in a ponytail. He had seen a lot of Peggy's body at the Club, but this was altogether new.

He noticed her breasts first, as always: they weren't as big as Kelly's, but big enough. Her nipples were erect and a little larger than Kelly's. *Women with larger breasts always seem to have smaller nipples, and vice versa*, he thought. Peggy's legs were very shapely and ended in a soft rounded ass. Her stomach was flat and showed no sign of fat anywhere. Her skin was golden brown with no tan lines: either she found time for a tanning bed or she sunbathed in the nude. *Interesting thought.*

"Come on in, I don't bite too much," Peggy said, smiling. She took her drink from Bryan's hand and sipped it. "I guess you didn't expect me to be dressed like this, did you? You made such a big fuss over my outfit at the Club—I thought I'd let you see the rest of the package."

Bryan was a little mystified. "You do have a gorgeous body. You should be proud!"

"Thank you, kind sir." She set her drink down on the night table and looked back at him. "Set your drink down and take your clothes off."

One invitation was enough; in seconds he stood naked before her. Peggy moved closer to him and rubbed the curly hair on his chest. Her hand stopped at his right nipple and pinched it. She reached her other hand up and lightly touched his cheek, bringing her soft, sensuous lips to his; he remembered those lips from the kiss she'd given him the night of the Level Three auction.

As their tongues touched and wove a magic course with their play, Bryan's flaccid cock responded and started to rise. Peggy slowly backed away and looked down at his manly hood. With a petite devil in her voice, she said, "Not bad, Bryan, not bad at all. In fact, you're truly a gorgeous hunk of a man."

"I'm a guy just like any other, you know, and we're easy."

She wrapped her velvety right hand around his thick shaft and worked it up and down a few times, then lightly rubbed the purple head of his cock. Soft moans escaped Bryan's mouth with each stroke. "Damn, that's good," he sputtered, his breath slightly labored.

Peggy stopped stroking his cock. "Lie down in the middle of the bed and put your head on the pillow," she commanded.

Bryan didn't want her to stop, but he followed her instructions. When he was lying down, she took a small scented towel, folded it in half, and placed it over his closed eyes to blindfold him.

"Lie still now," Peggy whispered sensuously. She took his left arm and guided it up over his head; then he felt her buckle a leather cuff around his wrist. She moved to the other side of the bed and repeated the same procedure with his right arm and wrist.

Bryan twisted in the bed, but offered little resistance. This was something new for him; he had always been the one doing the tying up.

She secured his ankles in the same fashion as his wrists. As Peggy was buckling the left ankle cuff, Bryan felt a second pair of hands delicately brush his left leg and realized that another person was in the room. He jerked his body, but to no avail: his restraints held tight.

"Open your mouth, dear Bryan, my lovely hunk of man," Peggy said, sitting down on the bed next to his head. At first, he didn't do it; he was enjoying Peggy's womanly smell.

Then she pinched his right nipple again. "*Aow!*" he blurted out, and at that instant, Peggy pushed a ball gag into his open mouth beyond his teeth.

"It's not nice to disobey my instructions, Bryan," she said. "You could be punished for that." Her voice softly echoed through Bryan's confused brain, still sensuous but now with an air of firmness. He felt the other person tighten the leather strap behind his head to hold the gag in place.

After a moment, Peggy removed the towel from Bryan's eyes. The room was dimly lit, and it took a few seconds for his eyes to focus. To his astonishment, Pat Howard was standing by the bed with Peggy, dressed in the same black leather outfit she'd worn at the Level Three auction.

"Surprise!" Pat said with a devilish smile. "I wanted you the first time I saw you at the Castaway Club. I knew you were worth it, especially after seeing that delicious hard-on of yours go into Alice's mouth. Just look at that cock, Peggy. Get a ruler. I bet that piece of meat is eight inches long."

Peggy opened the dresser drawer, pulled out a twelve-inch wooden ruler, and handed it to Pat. She put her hand around his cock and pulled it straight out from his body so Pat could measure it.

"Yep, I was right—the Pete Meter reads eight inches," said Pat. Putting the ruler down, she picked up two leather straps from the dresser table. "Do you know what these are for, my big boy?" she asked, holding up the leather straps.

Bryan shook his head, but he knew all too well what she was going to do.

"Well, then, let me show you. It gets me so horny doing this." Pat grabbed his balls and tightly squeezed them at the base of his shaft.

His balls hardened in pain. "*Ugh!*" he moaned through the gag.

Pat looped one of the straps tightly around his balls several times and tied it off. Then she wrapped the other strap around the base of his cock and pulled it tight.

"*UGH!*" Again, Bryan tried to scream behind the ball gag, but not much came out.

Pat looked at her handiwork and nodded. "That's good, real good and tight. The reason for this, Bryan, is to trap the blood in your cock and balls so they will stay amazingly hard forever." She giggled, then turned to Peggy. "Are you ready, my dear?"

"Yes, Mistress," Peggy replied. "I'm ready, but only if you are."

"Take that damn G-string off, then. It should've been off a long time ago." Pat's face took on an expression of authority.

While Peggy removed her G-string, Bryan looked into Pat's eyes. Her affectionate but haunting eyes told the story of a woman deep in desire, looking to travel to another solar system and take everyone with her.

"Do you remember, dear boy, in your office that day, I told you I had a stable of three women and two men that service me on a regular basis?" Pat asked. "Well, one of them is my lovely slave Peggy. She's such a slut—I just love her to death, especially when she eats me out. You already know Alice, and the third woman is Carol, the young feline at the front desk. They're all exquisitely submissive to my desires. I love them so much." Pat paused.

"Now, my precious little lapdog Peggy and I are going to play with you and that splendid hunk of meat of yours for a while. There are some rules to follow, so listen up—you know how I like to play games. Just remember, don't come until I tell you. If you do, keep in mind that I know how to handle a whip. When it's time for you to shoot your wad, I'll let you know."

Peggy sat down on the bed next to Pat and embraced her. Their lips met, and as they kissed, Bryan could see their tongues lapping at each other like two dogs in heat. Pat ended the kiss and forced Peggy to her knees. "Slave Peggy," she ordered, "put your head on his stomach and get a good look at that glorious cock."

Peggy did so, leaving her mouth only inches from the head of his throbbing cock. It needed some relief, any relief, as far as Bryan was concerned. Peggy's ass and pussy were now wide open for Pat, who took a position behind her. She unbuckled a tiny leather whip from her belt and struck Peggy's ass. "*Whack! Whack! Whack!*" The sound of raw leather strapping Peggy's gorgeous ass echoed through the quiet room.

"*Damn!*" Peggy cried as her body contorted under the wicked whip. She tossed her head from side to side, rubbing Bryan's stomach, and his cock bobbed like a cork on a fishing line. He could feel the strokes of the whip through Peggy's body. His cock was about to explode, but he remembered what Pat had told him: don't come until instructed. His sexual frustration was evident, but he could do nothing about it.

"*Whack! Whack! Whack!*" The whip sounded again against Peggy's bare flesh, harder this time. Her body jerked violently and red lines appeared on her ass cheeks. Aflame with desperate feminine desire, her pussy glistened in the soft light as her womanly juices cascaded down her thighs. After the last torturous cut from Pat's whip, Peggy squealed, "I'm ready! *Please,* Mistress, I'm ready!"

Pat marveled at the red lines across Peggy's inflamed ass. She knew Peggy's pussy was on fire and it needed to be extinguished. "My, my, delicious pet, you're such a pleasure slut," she said. Laying the whip down, she slid a finger into her slave's sex. "Yes, oh, my dear, I think you're ready. It's almost like an ocean down there. You're just a little minx, aren't you?"

Peggy stood up and Pat helped her straddle Bryan, her knees on either side of his pelvis and her pussy just below his cock. "Now, my dear," Pat instructed her, "put your hands behind you." Pat took a small length of rope, wrapped it several times around Peggy's wrists, and tied it tightly. She then moved to Peggy's front and kissed her again.

After the kiss, Peggy pushed herself up with her knees and Pat guided Bryan's very hard cock into her vagina. She slid down on Bryan, and a second later his cock had totally disappeared inside her.

Peggy began to move up and down on his cock, and Bryan moaned behind the ball gag, showing his teeth. Meanwhile, Pat removed her leather mistress suit and stood naked beside the bed watching them. She began to masturbate her own pussy. Bryan caught sight of the display and felt like he was in heaven. "*Gahh!*" Peggy gasped, breathing hard as she thrust herself up and down on Bryan's cock. Bryan arched his back and his head sank into the pillow.

Pat moved in to straddle Bryan's chest, facing Peggy, with her ass just in front of Bryan's face. The two women's knees touched as they kissed again, moving up and down together while Peggy rode Bryan's cock.

Pat kissed and bit each of Peggy's nipples, once and then again, and Bryan felt Peggy change her movements slightly in response. The heat of

Pat's pussy on his chest was almost equal to that of Peggy's pussy on his cock.

Suddenly, Peggy's body stiffened. Pat and Bryan could both feel it—in different ways, but they both knew. "*Gahhhh!*" Peggy cried out as the floodgates opened and her body released its river of desire onto Bryan's cock. The climax of this masterful fuck made her stop breathing for a few seconds. Her body jerked and shook; sweat poured from her cleavage and her face.

After Peggy recovered, she pulled away from Bryan's cock, slid off the bed, and sat down in the small dressing table chair, her hands still tied behind her back.

Pat immediately climbed over Bryan to replace Peggy in the same position. Bryan could feel the searing flesh of her vagina slide down his hard shaft and watched as his cock disappeared into her depths.

"Damn, that's good," Pat groaned. She squeezed her knees against Bryan's ass, her pussy lips around his cock, and held it there for several minutes. Then she began to ride his cock like a woman possessed. Soon, her body stiffened like Peggy's and a torrent of nectar from the gods came down.

Pat moved off the bed a few minutes' later and untied Peggy's hands. Bryan's cock was still rock-hard, with the leather straps still in place and doing their job. He hadn't had an orgasm yet, and he wasn't sure whether that meant he was lucky or not.

Peggy and Pat joined Bryan on the bed with their heads just inches from his bobbing cock. "Okay, Peggy, you first," Pat told her. Peggy looked at Pat, smiled her devilish smile, and licked Bryan's shaft from balls to head. She repeated this several times, then took his cock into her mouth and began to move her head up and down.

Bryan could only muster a grunt from behind the gag. "*Ugh!*" His cock was hurting so badly, all he wanted to do was come, but that was not to be just yet. After several more strokes of Peggy's tongue and lips on Bryan's cock, Pat pushed her away and replaced Peggy's mouth with her own. While Pat was trying to swallow Bryan's cock, Peggy bent down to Bryan's chest and licked the sweat away. He could only lie there and accept the attentions of the two talented women.

Finally, Pat stopped her oral attack on Bryan's cock and nudged Peggy. "It's time, baby," she said. Peggy grabbed Bryan's balls and Pat grabbed the base of his cock, and both women started to massage him at the same time. "Okay, Bryan, it's your turn," Pat said, smiling at him.

Together they said, "*COME!*" Bryan arched his back; his cock moved skyward. His body tensed and he stopped breathing for a few seconds. Drool oozed from the side of his gag. "*Gahh! Gahh!*" he tried to scream. The massage continued, and seconds later, an explosion erupted from the massive tormented head of his cock. His cum shot twelve inches into the air and landed on his stomach.

"My God!" Peggy exclaimed. "I've never seen a man shoot his cum that high."

"Wow!" Pat said. "You're right, what a sight!"

Bryan arched his back and his head got lost in the pillow. "*Gahh!*" Another cry came from his gagged mouth as another shot erupted from his cock. This load was not as strong as before: it only went only a few inches into the air and landed on his pubic hair.

"Would you look at that, Pat?" Peggy said in amazement. "Never does a man shoot off twice like that."

Bryan settled back down on the bed and started to breathe again, cum oozing from the head of his cock. Pat moved to Bryan's stomach and started licking away the spent cum while Peggy licked his shaft and the head of his cock.

Several minutes later, the women had finished licking all of the cum from Bryan's body. They got off the bed and looked at him; he lay there like a little whipped puppy,

still tied down.

Peggy picked up the towel, replaced it over Bryan's eyes, and used some tape to keep it in place. "Bryan, my dear Bryan, get a good night's sleep. I'll see you in the morning." With that, she and Pat left the bedroom. Before Peggy closed the door, she switched the light off.

The Kidnapping (Chapter 12)

Early the next morning, Peggy entered her bedroom, where Bryan still lay in much the same position as when she left. She removed the towel from his eyes and undid the gag and the rest of the restraints, then told him to take a shower and get dressed and breakfast would be ready when he finished.

On the ride back to Bryan's condo, their conversation centered on the events of the past night. "Peggy, this is the first time I've ever had things done to me like that," Bryan said. "You set me up! I didn't know you belonged to Pat."

"I always wanted to be submissive to another woman," she answered. "It was a fantasy of mine ever since I found out what sex was all about. It's extremely exciting to be under another woman's control." Peggy paused to look over at him. "Pat wanted to play with you, and actually, I did too. You see, I love men as well. You're a very handsome man, and any woman would enjoy your ability to please her. I've never been so turned on in my life, and from the looks of things, you got into the act as well."

"Yes, I truly did," he remarked. "I've never been tied up like that before, and it was certainly a learning experience. You and Pat are both ravishing women. I have to say, Pike's Point Italian is by far the best I've ever had; Rome would be envious."

"You're nuts, you know that?" Peggy giggled as Bryan got out of her car in front of his apartment. She waved. "See you at work on Monday!"

Later that afternoon, Bryan dressed and headed to the golf club restaurant for his evening meal. To his surprise, Bill was there having dinner with Kelly, Virginia, Frank, and Frank's lovely wife.

"May I join you folks?" he asked, approaching their table.

"Hey there, Bryan!" Bill said, gesturing for him to sit down. "By all means! I'm glad you're here. You're in for a treat tonight. After dinner, Christy Wells is going to put on a little show and do some singing; she's quite good."

Bryan sat down next to Kelly, who was looking as stunning as ever. Dinner was great, and afterwards, everybody sat back to watch and listen to the gorgeous and charming Christy Wells. She walked onstage with her small band and began to sing.

Bryan whispered in Kelly's ear, "That's Kim!"

Kelly smiled and whispered back, "No, it's Christy, but they do look a lot alike, don't they?"

"My God! Yes, they do." Bryan was stunned at how closely the singer resembled Kim.

"Christy has sung here several times," Kelly informed him. "We put her and Kim side by side once; they're not twins, but they could easily be sisters. The main difference between them is that Christy can sing—Kim can't carry a note in a bucket," she laughed.

The show lasted about an hour and a half, and the audience seemed thrilled with Christy and her group. When it was over, the two older couples said their good-byes, leaving Kelly and Bryan at the table.

"Bryan," Kelly suggested, "What do you say we go check on Peggy and Kim at the Club? Sometimes things get busy after Christy sings. People like her show, but afterwards they drift down to the Club for more drinks. Peggy and Kim may need my help."

As Kelly and Bryan made their way through the parking lot toward the Club, a large black car with its lights off sped by. Bryan grabbed Kelly's arm just in time to keep the car from hitting her.

"That was close!" Bryan exclaimed, giving the car a dirty look. "That guy's crazy or something—he needs to slow that damned thing down. You okay?" he asked, helping her to her feet.

"Yeah, I'm okay," Kelly answered, brushing off her clothes.

They watched the black car pull up near the rear entrance to the main clubhouse, where Christy and her drummer were standing on the sidewalk talking. Two men jumped out of the car. One of them pulled out a handgun and pistol-whipped the drummer in the face, knocking him to the sidewalk.

"Kelly!" Bryan whispered, excited. "Did you see that? He hit that guy in the face with a gun!"

"Yes, I did, keep quiet!" Kelly whispered harshly. "Get down so they won't see us!" They huddled down behind a car and watched.

"You bastard!" Kelly and Bryan heard Christy scream. The second guy grabbed her and forced a white rag over her face. Christy tried to fight, but she was no match for him. Within seconds, she slumped in his arms.

"It's got to be chloroform or something like that," Kelly whispered. They continued to watch as the two men threw Christy's limp body in the back seat of the car, closed the door, and drove away with their victim.

"Bryan, get some help for the drummer! I've got to follow these people!" Kelly's voice and attitude changed as she scrambled towards her car.

"No way!" said Bryan. "I'm not gonna let you go after those bastards by yourself."

"Get in the car, then!" she called back to him.

Bryan jumped in. Kelly switched her headlights off and followed the black car, racing down the golf course road toward the highway entrance. The black car sped by the security station and onto the main highway. Bryan could hear the screeching tires as the car headed toward the city.

Kelly reached between the front seats and picked up her mobile phone, pushed a button, and waited for the phone to connect. "Peggy, this is Kelly!" she said. "Two guys have just kidnapped Christy Wells from the parking lot at the Club. Bryan and I saw it. We're following these bastards." She paused. "Bryan wouldn't let me go alone. I guess he's got a death wish. Get somebody to help the drummer—he was attacked—and call Bill. Tell him to get the troops together. When I find out where they're going, I'll let you know."

Kelly put the telephone down. *"Bryan!"* she screamed. "Don't let me lose this guy!"

"I've got an eye on him—just drive!" he said. The black car merged onto the interstate, heading toward the south of town and the warehouse area. Kelly followed.

"Okay, Kelly, tell me what's going on," said Bryan. "You're a cop or something, aren't you?"

"Or something," she replied, speeding through the merging traffic. "I guess you should know the whole story. For about a year and a half, young, beautiful professional women have been getting kidnapped from several points along the East Coast. Peggy and I were sent here to investigate."

"You mean you don't work for Bill?"

"Well, we do, but it's a cover. We actually work for a government agency," Kelly said. "Bill and Frank's company has been dealing with some very rich and powerful overseas clients. That's why they hired you: they needed the help.

"These kidnappers are actually placing orders for specific women. They're very dangerous people, and we've learned that their staging point for shipping women overseas is in this area. That's why I didn't try to stop them from taking Christy: we have to track them to their base of operations. I just hope she's okay."

Ten minutes later, the black car pulled off the interstate and stopped beside a chain-link fence at the entrance to a gravel road. "Kelly, the driver is looking to see if anybody is following him," Bryan said. "Pull into the gas station."

Kelly turned into the parking lot of the gas station across the street. Bryan got out and pretended to pump some gas. After a few minutes, the black car pulled off and continued down the gravel road. Bryan jumped back in and they continued to follow.

"That was a good idea, Bryan. Looks like you've done this before," Kelly said approvingly.

"Not really," he said. "Well, okay, maybe once, but the intrigue gets me turned on."

The black car came to a stop at a gate with a sign that read, "South Point Bonded Warehouses." The man in the passenger seat got out and unlocked the gate. The car proceeded through, the kidnapper put the lock back in place, and they traveled on.

Seconds later, Kelly drove up to the gate and stopped. "Open it, Bryan."

"It's locked!" he replied.

"Not really—it only looks that way," she told him. "I've been here before. Ted Darling took me out to eat a few times. On one of those dates, he told me he had to go check on one of his men, that he provided security for these warehouses. He brought me in this way."

Bryan opened the gate and they followed the road to the end of the row of warehouses. Bryan could see Kelly's face flush red with anger in the faint light of the car's dashboard. "That son of a bitch! The car went into Warehouse B-4. That's the one Ted went into. There's a back entrance."

Kelly drove her car behind Warehouse B-5 and stopped in the dark, next to the fence overlooking a back door. "Look in the glove compartment," she said. Bryan opened the small door and pulled out two nine-millimeter handguns. "Do you know how to use one of these?" she asked.

"Yes, I do," he said.

Kelly took one of the guns and slid a clip into the chamber. Bryan copied her move.

"Don't use it unless you have to, but if you have to, just do it, understand?" Kelly warned. "These guys will kill first and ask questions later. Let's go."

They stayed close to the buildings for cover and made their way to a small door at the back of Warehouse B-4. Kelly bent down and retrieved a key from under a loose rock at the foot of the door. "I saw Ted do this that night," she said. She eased the key into the lock and slowly opened the creaking door.

The smell of mold erupted from inside as they slipped into the dark warehouse and shut the door. Slowly they made their way through the maze of shipping containers and wooden crates labeled "TONY REMA SHIPPING." In the distance, they heard voices coming from the small lighted window of an office.

Kelly and Bryan located a secure place between the crates where they could watch and hear what the kidnappers were saying. Just to the side of the office, they saw the black car they had been following.

Kelly looked at Bryan, their faces only inches apart. She whispered, "Be quiet—our lives depend on it. And stay in the dark. We can't let them know we're here!"

Ted Darling was standing outside the office with the two kidnappers. "Mick, is she awake?" he asked.

"She's coming around," one of the men said.

"Jake, help Mick, let's get her out here." Ted carried a chair from the office and put it by the door. Christy stumbled as they escorted her to the chair, still under the influence of the chloroform, her arms hanging at her sides like a little rag doll. She sat down with her head bent, a curtain of hair hiding her face and chest.

"Well, my dear Kim, I hope you enjoyed your little nap?" Ted stood over her and smiled.

Christy slowly raised her head and looked up. Her voice was weak and slurred. "My—name's—not—Kim. My name is Christy, *Christy Wells*."

Ted took a picture out of his pocket and compared it to her face. "Looks like Kim to me. You work the bar at the Club, don't you?"

"I—I only sing with my band at the main clubhouse from time to time." Her voice was quavering, but gaining a little strength. "You've got the wrong woman. Kim, I do know her, and we look a lot alike. She's the one you want, not me. Does this mean you'll let me go?"

Ted stared at the picture, then at her. "Mr. Rema wants the woman named Kim. He feels he paid enough for her at that Level Three auction," he remarked to his two accomplices.

"Here, boss, check this out," Mick said. "It was in her pocket." He handed Christy's wallet to Ted.

"Boys," Ted said, inspecting her ID, "I think she's telling the truth. This isn't Kim. Her hair's too long anyway." He turned to Christy. "Well, my dear, to answer your question, no. You were in the wrong place at the wrong time. My guys just made a mistake."

Ted glanced back at the two thugs. "Mr. Rema will not be a happy camper. I guess I'll just have to give him this one as a present. We'll get that Kim girl in due time."

Kelly and Bryan looked at each other, in shock at what they had just heard.

"Well, Christy," Ted continued, "we all have choices in life, and you're about to make one. Before you join our little group, you'll have to remove your clothes—all of them. You won't be needing them anymore, especially where you're going. Here's your choice: either you take them off yourself or my two guys here will do it for you. You decide."

Christy hesitated, giving him a desperate look.

Ted shook his head. "What's it gonna be?"

Reluctantly, Christy unbuttoned her shirt and took off her bra, along with her shoes and socks. She eased her slacks down her long, slender legs, and Ted finished it by pulling her panties off. She stood awkwardly before the men, completely naked.

Her nicely shaped breasts rose and fell as she tried to control her breathing. Her nipples were erect and stood at attention, awaiting her uncertain fate. Her black pubic hair was short, but still covered most of her slit.

Ted made her turn around and admired her splendidly rounded ass. "Just right for a good fuck and whipping. You're real pretty, you know that? I know Rema wants that Kim, but I don't think he'll be too unhappy," Ted assured her as he patted her ass.

The drug was wearing off, and Christy was beginning to understand what was happening to her. "You're disgusting people! I hope you all burn in hell!" she cried, her voice gaining strength and defiance.

"I might," Ted said. "If I do, I know where you're going. And who knows, I might even see you there!"

Mick pulled Christy's hands behind her back and secured her wrists with a pair of handcuffs. Jake put leather cuffs on her ankles and secured them with a two-foot length of chain.

"That's so you can walk, but you won't go too far too fast," Ted informed her.

"Why are you doing this to me?" she begged. "Please, I haven't done anything to you."

"You're one of the chosen, my dear lady, and who knows how much money you might be worth?" Ted replied.

Mick wrapped a leather collar around her neck and locked it in place with a small padlock.

"One last thing, Christy. Open that lovely mouth of yours." Ted showed her the red ball gag.

"I will *not!*" she screamed. "You're not putting that raunchy thing in my mouth!"

Ted pulled a hand whip from his back pocket and struck her just above her pussy. "*Ahee!*" she yelled, bending over at the waist.

A second stroke, a little lower this time, the whip caught her full on her slit.

"*Ahee!*" She yelled again. She tried to run, but the chain between her ankle cuffs tripped her up. She raised her head from her bent position as red lines appeared on her skin. The savage pain on her face was quite evident.

"Mick, would you like to feel that pretty body of hers get spanked?" Ted asked his assistant.

"Damned right I would, boss," Mick said approvingly.

"Sit in the chair, and when she's lying across your lap, pull her hands up as high as you can." As Ted forced Christy down over Mick's lap, Mick pulled her arms up behind her by the handcuffs, the metal cutting deep into her wrists.

"Mick, keep her hands high now," Ted said. "Christy, it's best you understand that when you're told to do something, you do it, and you don't ask questions."

Whack! Ted's whip ripped a punishing stroke across her exposed ass. Her body jerked, but she was held tight by Mick's right hand.

"*Ahee!* That hurts! Please, no more. Please! *Please, I beg you!*" Christy was almost in tears from the searing, penetrating pain of Ted's whip.

"Mick, hold her tight." *Whack*! Ted struck her ass again and Mick stared at the red lines appearing on her exquisite backside. Holding her arms with one hand and her back with the other, he could feel every jerk when the whip struck.

Whack! The third strike almost caused Mick to lose his grip on Christy as she threw her head to one side, her hair flying. "*Ugh!*" she cried. "I'll do anything you ask! Please, please, no more!"

"Stand her up, Mick." Ted dangled the gag in front of her face again as Mick allowed her to stand up. She opened her mouth, and Ted inserted the gag behind her teeth. Mick buckled the straps behind her head.

"Jake, take her downstairs and lock her up with the others. I'll be down shortly," Ted ordered. "Mick, seal the car up in one of the shipping containers. We don't want that car on the road for a while."

Jake grabbed Christy by the arm and tugged her toward a small stairwell behind the office. The chain kept her from moving very quickly. Jake just took her arm and ushered her along.

Bryan couldn't take his eyes off Christy and her lovely red ass. She was a beautiful woman, and under better circumstances, she might be a lot of fun.

Kelly whispered in Bryan's ear, "He's a real bastard, isn't he? Okay, enough looking, get your mind back on business. Let's go."

She touched his shoulder as they picked their way to the back of the warehouse. "I saw a stairwell as we came in that might lead to that basement. I want to see where that guy is taking her."

Bryan followed her down the back stairs and through an unlocked wooden door. The basement was just as dark and moldy as the floor above, with more boxes and containers lining the cold cement floor. Another small lighted office window in the distance gave enough light for them to maneuver by. They made their way through the aisles to the other side of the warehouse.

To the right of the office, next to the wall, they could see Jake-dragging Christy to a large cage with figures moving around inside. "Look, Bryan!" Kelly whispered, pointing to the cage. After a closer look, he realized there were four other naked women in restraints just like the ones Christy was wearing. Jake pushed Christy in and locked the door.

Ted joined Jake in the basement a few minutes later, and both men walked over to a large container just beyond the cage. "Hey, Maze, how's it going in there?" Ted asked, sticking his head through the container door.

Maze stepped out of the container and wiped his hands on a rag. "Just a few more minutes, boss, and that false wall you wanted will be done. If you look at it, it just looks like a lot of boxes stacked up. There's enough room for your four women, and I've added more space for the cargo." He gestured back into the container. "I put some air holes in so we won't lose anybody, but you'll have to keep their gags in place. With the air holes in the wall, somebody might hear one of them scream or something. After I finish the wall, it will take about twenty minutes to load the rest of the crates and we can leave."

"That's great," Ted said, "but you mean five women, don't you?" He pointed to the cage.

Maze looked to Ted, then the cage. He chuckled and shook his head. "Got another one. Man, you're good."

"The *Colotta* will be putting out to sea just as soon as we can load this container and get it on the ship," Ted told Maze.

"Okay, boss. I'll use the hoist to pick up the container and then lock it on the flatbed before I load those crates with the lift."

"Just be very careful," Ted informed him. "We don't want anything to happen to those crates painted with the two and three red dots."

"The women can go in before I put the container on the flatbed," Maze said. "Let me finish the wall—I'm gonna have to add some more hooks. You keep bringing in more women!"

Ted walked back to the office and sat down at the desk.

Kelly's Torment (Chapter 13)

Kelly lightly touched Bryan's shoulder again and whispered in his ear. "Bryan, let's go. We've got to get back to the car. I've got to call Peggy and Bill and let them know what's going on."

Within a few minutes they were back in Kelly's car. Kelly called Peggy on her cell phone. "Listen up, Peggy," she said, talking and trying to evaluate their situation at the same time. "We're at the warehouses south of the city, Warehouse B-4. In the basement, these bastards have five naked kidnapped women locked in some ratty cages. They're going to be locked in container 2150-B and transported to a ship named the *Colotta.*"

Kelly continued, a little excited that they had found out so much information, "Rema wanted Kim and not Christy. I heard Ted Darling say Rema had paid too much for her at the auction and she belonged to him, for real. You'd better have Kim picked up. I don't know how many more of those bastards might be out there looking for her."

"Tell Bill that Ted Darling is right smack in the middle of this thing and this is the break we've been waiting for. I'm going back into the warehouse—I want to be there when you guys get here. These men are armed and very dangerous, but maybe I can protect the women. The cages are at the north end of the warehouse. Bryan is going to stay with the car."

Kelly put down the phone and turned to Bryan, who was astounded at what he had just heard. "She'll be here with Bill in twenty minutes. Here are the car keys. If things go south, you get the hell out of here, you understand?"

Bryan hesitated. "You sure you really want to do this?"

"Not really," she shrugged, her face blank, "but it's my job."

Bryan could see a haunting, aggressive, violent look on her face, one he had never seen before. He held up the gun and showed it to her. "I'll be okay. You watch your ass! I might want to spank it again sometime."

Kelly gave him a faint smile. "You're such a bad boy, you know that? But I love you anyway. I'll be back in a few minutes."

Bryan watched as she eased the car door shut and cautiously approached the warehouse door. As she started to open it, a man pushed the door open and it hit her, knocking her to the ground. It was Mick! He grabbed Kelly, put a gun to her head, and forced her to follow him into the warehouse.

Desperate to get to Kelly, Bryan left the car and hurried to the same warehouse door, opened it, and eased inside. He could hear a commotion coming from the bottom of the basement stairs: Kelly was giving Mick a hard time. *Be very careful, Kelly*, he thought, *that bastard just might shoot and ask questions later.*

Bryan followed Mick and Kelly across the warehouse aisle and through the maze of shipping crates, making sure no one saw him. He could still see the fire in Kelly's eyes: Mick's gun under her chin was the only thing that kept her under control. When he reached the same vantage point that he and

Kelly had vacated earlier, he sat down silently in the dark to watch and listen.

"Hey! Boss! Got a present for you!" Mick bellowed toward Ted, who was sitting behind a metal desk in the small office. He pushed Kelly toward the door, her head up and turned to one side from the force of the gun.

"What the hell is this?" Ted asked. He looked Kelly up and down, admiring the strained position she was in. "Well, I'll be damned! My dear Kelly, what are you doing here?"

Before she could answer, Mick held up Kelly's gun. "She had this on her, boss, and she tried to get in the back door."

Trying to sound convincing, Kelly said, "You weren't at the Club tonight and I wanted to see you." .

"So you came here?" Ted seemed amused, knowing she was full of shit but interested to see where the conversation would go.

"That's right," she said. "You brought me here once—remember, when you took me out to dinner that time and you got a call to check on one of your guys?"

"What were you going to do, shoot me or something? It seems a little strange for someone wanting to see me," Ted asked, inspecting her gun. "I might have believed you, except for one thing: this gun of yours is military issue. Who are you working for? You a cop or something?"

Kelly could see that Ted's expression and demeanor had changed. The penetrating stare he gave her was from the devil. She said nothing.

"Why don't you have a seat on this crate, my dear?" Ted said. He held her gun up to the light and turned it around. "Damn! That's a big gun!"

Kelly sat down.

"Mick, was there anyone else outside?" Ted asked.

"Didn't see anyone, boss," Mick replied, satisfied that he had done a good job for Ted.

"Better check around a bit. I'm sure her car is out there someplace, and somebody might be with her."

"Right, boss," Mick agreed. "If there's somebody out there, I'll get m'."

Jake came over and eyed Kelly, still sitting on the crate. "What are you gonna do with her?" he asked.

"I gotta find out what she knows," Ted said. "Some people have been asking a lot of questions about me lately, and she knows more than she's telling."

He turned back to Kelly. "Kelly, my haughty little bitch, as you can see, we're in the shipping business." He gestured toward the five naked women locked in the large cage. "You've been a lot of fun and you're a gorgeous piece of ass, so I guess you'll have to join our little group."

"Just like all the others," Ted continued, "you'll have to make a choice. Either you remove your clothes, all of them, or Jake here will take this gun and shoot a bunch of holes in that lovely body of yours. I'd hate to see that, but you're expendable: you haven't been paid for like these other women."

"You're a bastard, you know that?" Kelly raged.

"Yeah, some people have said that about me, but Rema, he's worse. Guess who you'll get to see?" Ted chuckled. "Now take them off and be quick about it!"

Bryan was powerless to do anything; all he could do was listen and watch from his hidden position.

Kelly removed her shirt and bra. "Nice tits," Jake said, delighted at seeing her chest exposed. Within a few seconds, she had removed the rest of her clothes, and her naked body was prominently displayed to both men.

"Is this what you want to see?" she barked at Ted. "My body on display for your glaring men? I hope they get a eyeful."

"Nice piece of ass. What do you think, Jake?" Ted still had the devil in his eyes.

Jake nodded. "I couldn't agree more." He roughly pulled her wrists behind her and handcuffed her, just as they had done to Christy. Ted took metal ankle cuffs and locked them around her ankles; a two-foot chain connected them. Jake stood behind her as Ted wrapped a black leather collar around her neck and locked it in place.

"Now, my dear," Ted said, glaring into her face with cold steel savage eyes, "I will torture it out of you if you don't tell me what I want to know. Who do you work for?"

Small beads of sweat appeared on Kelly's chest. She met his stare defiantly, like a lioness ready to strike a killing blow. "*Go to hell*, you son of a bitch!"

Ted smiled and slapped her face. Her head recoiled to one side, drool flying from her mouth. She immediately twisted back to face his torturous glare. He cupped and squeezed her left breast, then pinched her nipple. She jerked away from him and said through clenched teeth, "That's not gonna do any good."

"Jake, take her to the other side of the warehouse. I'll be right there." Ted returned to his office and Jake grabbed Kelly's arm. She was only able to take short steps because of the ankle chain, and it took them a few minutes to reach the other side of the warehouse. Soon Ted joined them, carrying several lengths of rope, some wire, and some tools.

Bryan shifted his position to a closer hiding place, but stayed out of sight in the dark.

He could only watch whatever they were going to do to Kelly. His previous BDSM experiences gave him an idea of what Ted had in mind; he was afraid it wouldn't be a fun time for her.

"Jake, sit her down and tie these ropes around her ankles," Ted said, unlocking Kelly's ankle chain. Jake followed Ted's instructions and tied a short length of rope around each ankle. Ted then unlocked her handcuffs and brought her hands back in front of her, and Jake tied another short length of rope around each wrist.

Ted pushed a button and a small engine sparked to life, lowering a cable from a hoist attached to a beam in the ceiling. Attached to the cable was a four-foot rod that descended to just above Kelly's chest. Ted tied Kelly's wrists to the ends of the rod, and Jake tied her ankles to another rod that was already positioned on the floor. Then Ted pushed the button again, raising Kelly's arms above her head. He stopped the hoist just before her feet left the floor.

Kelly was stretched in a spread-eagle stance, her pussy and ass wide open for whatever was to happen next. She arched her back to ease the strain, and her breasts heaved in and out with her labored breathing, nipples hard and fully erect. Both men stood there, fascinated by the sight of her glorious body.

"My, what a beautiful sight," Ted said approvingly.

Jake nodded as he stepped back. "She's a great piece of ass, isn't she?"

"She's still a bitch cop, though, and I want some answers!" Ted's menacing voice echoed off the warehouse walls.

Kelly didn't know what he intended to do to her, but she knew it wasn't going to be good. She eyed the tools and other things Ted had brought and hoped she could get through it.

"Kelly," Ted said, smiling at his helpless conquest, "it's up to you. We can just go back to the container and this will all be over if you tell me what

I want to know."

"Kiss my ass!" Kelly spat. "I won't tell you shit."

"Ah. Very well then, I guess we'll just see how much training you've had, won't we?" Ted took a piece of 14-gauge high-tension wire, wrapped it around her waist, and twisted the two ends together, tightening the wire with pliers until it sank deep into her skin. He snipped the jagged ends off, leaving only a small nub of wire visible.

"*Ow*! *Damn*! *Damn it*! That hurts, you're cutting me in half!" Kelly screamed, writhing from the searing pain around her middle. No matter how she turned, there was no relief from the wire.

Ted reached into his pocket and pulled out a cock-shaped dildo. It was almost as long as an average man's cock, but somewhat thinner. At the base, a small hole had been drilled through it. "Cute, isn't it?" he said mockingly. He looped a second wire around the waist wire just above the crack of Kelly's ass, twisted it tight, and fed the end of the wire through the hole in the dildo. "Now, my glorious bitch, I'm gonna stick this cute little butt plug up your ass."

"*No!*" Kelly shrieked, trying to turn her body away from him. Sweat started to roll down her cheeks and between her breasts.

"Hold her still, Jake, and spread her ass cheeks," Ted ordered. Without any lubricant, he jammed the plug into her ass until the only thing that was visible was the wire.

"No, please, Ted! *No!*" she screamed. "You're tearing me apart! My sphincter can't take this! *Please!*"

He pulled the wire through her pussy slit, fastened it to the waist wire in front, and cut off the end. The dildo was now tightly wired into her ass.

"Push the button, Jake," Ted instructed. Jake grabbed the control and engaged the hoist engine, raising Kelly's body until her feet were several inches from the floor. Then Ted took the whip from his back pocket and slashed her pussy with a solid blow.

"*Hahee!*" Kelly screamed, and her body jerked. Another slash. "*Hahee!*"

"Who do you work for, bitch?" Ted shouted. "Tell me what I want to know and this will stop."

She pulled her head up and glared at him. Spit flew out of her mouth as she yelled, "Go to hell, you son of a bitch!"

Ted slashed her pussy again with a punishing stroke. Kelly's screams echoed off the warehouse walls as the whipping continued for several minutes. Red marks and welts lined Kelly's inner thighs, and more sweat was running down her chest as she desperately tugged at her rope restraints.

"Jake, hold her body still. Her jerking and swinging is out of control. I want her still so she can feel this," Ted said. Then he shouted, "Tell me to go to hell again, *bitch!*" and resumed his brutal assault on Kelly's wired pussy. He was like a man possessed, almost out of control.

After several more strokes of the whip, she lost consciousness. Ted stopped his vicious whipping and casually retrieved a cup of water from a water cooler next to the warehouse wall. He returned to the unconscious Kelly and threw the water in her face.

She shook her head and opened her eyes as the cold water ran down her face and between her breasts. "Works every time, Jake," Ted said, a smile appearing on his devil face. "Kelly, my dear Kelly, you are such a pleasure, and that lovely body of yours just hanging there, totally helpless. You know, this is escape-proof and we can go on for a very long time—all night long if we have to. It's your choice. Now who do you work for? ATF? CIA? FBI? Are you a U.S. Marshal? Who is it, Kelly?"

Kelly started to lift her head. Ted helped her by roughly grabbing her hair and pulling her head up to face him. Drool oozed from the side of her mouth, and she could hardly speak. She whispered, "All of 'em."

"All of them? You say, all of them?" Ted looked mystified. He let go of her hair and her head fell forward. She hung in her restraints like a rag doll, water dripping to the floor from her body.

"Jake, looks like the feds are onto our operation," he said. "Let's get her down and chained up, get the rest of the women and the crates, and get them in the container. Maze and I will go to the ship with the container. You and Mick start moving the rest of the two-and three-dot crates to the warehouse in Atlanta. We'll set up again in a few weeks—it'll take us that long to get back from the delivery."

Ted helped Jake untie Kelly and lift her over his shoulder. Jake carried her to the container, removed all the ropes, then cuffed and chained her like the other women and inserted a ball gag in her mouth.

Bryan followed them back through the maze of containers and crates to his original hidden position. *I must admit, Kelly was an incredible sight in suspension,* he thought. *I'll have to remember that.*

As Ted headed back into his office, Jake asked him, "Boss, what about the wire and her ass plug?" Kelly was starting to come back to herself, but didn't have the strength to put up much resistance.

"Leave it in her ass," Ted called from the office door. "She'd better get used to it. They've got a name for it where's she's going—they call it anal training."

"All right, bring her in!" Maze said from inside the container. Jake pulled Kelly to her feet and helped her stumble between the crates in the container. He forced her through a door to the back wall of the container.

Maze instructed, "Make her face toward the back of the container. Pull her arms and wrists up and chain the cuffs to the hook in the ceiling—it'll make her bend real far forward at the waist." Maze showed Jake how he had the hooks and the false door set up.

"I see what you mean—totally escape-proof, and man, it has to be a strain on the body," Jake commented. He finished pulling Kelly's wrists and arms up above her head and attaching them the ceiling hook. "Oh! Ted said you were gonna go to the ship with him and Mick and I would be moving the main crates to Atlanta."

Maze gave him a worried look. "Just you be damned careful. That's a lot of high explosives you're gonna be dealing with, especially that one over there. You see the one that's labeled with the four red dots on it and the big 25-C?"

"Yeah, I see it, want to tell me about it?" Jake looked a little uneasy at the prospect of dealing with so many explosives.

"It's 25 pounds of C-4. No caps around it, but you'd better be careful with that one."

"I understand. I'll be careful," Jake said.

Kelly's wrists and arms were cuffed behind her and hooked to the ceiling, and each ankle cuff was hooked to the floor. Maze admired his handiwork. "Not bad," he told Jake. "She can't move in any direction."

"I like the look!" Jake said. He went back for another woman and forced her to the back of the container behind Kelly. Maze grabbed her cuffed wrists and hooked them to the ceiling, forcing her to bend at the waist and her head to rest on Kelly's back. Jake secured the second woman's ankle cuffs to another floor hook.

After they finished securing the remaining women in the container, Maze said, "They look like a bunch of sardines in a can." Then he closed the door and locked it. "No one inspecting this container will be able to tell this is a false door."

Bryan could see all six women chained and bent over in the back of the container as Maze sealed the door. All he could think about was how roughly Kelly had been treated. Where was Peggy with the troops?

Maze connected the four chains that surrounded the container to a massive ceiling hook and hoist. He hoisted the container high enough to back the diesel truck and flatbed under it, lowered the container onto the flatbed, and locked it down.

Ted returned from his office with two gym bags and a briefcase and set them on the floor. "Maze, when you get the crates loaded, stuff these two gym bags into a washing machine in one of the regular crates and tape the door shut."

Wiping his hands on a rag, Maze walked to the container doors and stood beside Ted.

"I've finished locking the container to the flatbed. Jake told me I was going to the ship with you."

Ted walked around the flatbed and examined Maze's handiwork. "Yep, I'm gonna need your help on this one. We've got four women already on board ship, and this will make ten."

"That's right, we took 2150-A to the *Colotta* a couple of days ago. Can you give me a little heads up as to what's gonna happen?"

"Sure, why not?" Ted smiled. "It's really simple. Once this container is on board, the *Colotta* will weigh anchor, and two days from now we'll meet up with a diesel submarine. It'll be Rema."

"A submarine?" Maze asked, incredulous.

"That's right. He bought one from Libya about two years ago in one hell of a gun deal. We'll supply the sub with food, fuel, and all the other things it needs. Rema has twenty mercenaries running it for him." Ted gestured toward the large crates next to the container. "Those crates with the three red dots are holding six torpedoes. Last month they blew up a merchant ship and they're out of ammo.

"The women and the small arsenal we have on the *Colotta* will be transferred to the sub at sea. The *Colotta* will continue to her port of call in England, but she'll be a clean ship when she gets there; everything will match the paperwork. After the inspection, she'll be loaded with import merchandise to return to the States."

"Okay, what happens to us?"

Ted looked at his watch. "Time's getting short. We'll stay on the sub and continue to a private island near the coast of Greece, where the women will be offloaded. The island has a small airfield, and their new owners will fly in to pick up the women.

"From there, the sub will dock at a submarine pen just off the mainland. Actually, it's a big cave; the Germans used it during World War II. The weapons and ammo to be sold will be unloaded into four trucks. Mr. Rema will escort the trucks to a hidden place in the desert to meet the buyer."

"What about the last two women you brought in here? No one's bought them yet," Maze asked.

Ted smiled. "Not to worry. Rema will take them to the desert and work out a deal with the people buying the weapons—he always does. Okay, let's get this container finished."

Bryan was very concerned now. He knew their plans, but Peggy, Bill, and the troops had not shown up to raid the place. He eased back through the maze of containers, out of the warehouse, and back toward Kelly's car, staying in the shadows because he knew Mick was out there somewhere. As he approached the car, he saw Mick bending over and peering in the driver's side window. Bryan was only a few feet away from him. He jingled the car keys. "Looking for these?"

Mick turned around and took a swing at him. Bryan ducked and hit Mick on the left side of the face with his gun. A thud softly echoed through the trees as Mick slumped over the hood of the car and his unconscious body came to rest on the ground. "That's for Kelly, you bastard!"

Looking around, Bryan saw a large box sitting beside the dock to Warehouse B-5. He grabbed Mick by the shoulders, pulled him across the driveway, and opened the lid. The metal box was empty, so he dumped Mick inside, closed the lid, and used a small piece of wood from a broken pallet to secure the latch. He stood back, wiped his hands, and admired his admired his handiwork.

Seconds later, the large cargo door of Warehouse B-4 opened and the diesel truck roared out of the building with its container 2150-B.

The Rescue (Chapter 14)

Bryan eased Kelly's car between the warehouses with the lights off and followed the truck onto the interstate, heading south.

Redial on Kelly's phone, and almost instantly, Peggy answered, screaming, "Where the *hell* are you, Kelly?"

Bryan spoke into the phone, trying to keep calm as he continued to follow a short distance behind the truck. "Peggy, it's not Kelly, it's Bryan. They got her."

"What the *hell* do you mean they got her?"

"Peggy, she went back into the warehouse to wait for you guys, but one of Ted Darling's men came from the inside and knocked her down. She's now one of the kidnapped."

Bill came on the line. "Where are you now, Bryan?"

"Hey, Bill. Kelly is chained in the back of a ship's container on a flatbed truck along with five other women. I'm following them on the interstate heading south toward the docks. Where are you guys? I waited for you and you didn't show up."

"The warehouses south of the city. *Damn it!*" Peggy broke in. "We went to the north warehouses."

"Peggy," Bryan replied, "we were at the south warehouses. She told you, south of the city!"

"Bryan, both sets of warehouses are south of the city," she said.

"That answers that question, I guess," he said.

"Okay, Bryan, you still following the truck?" Bill asked.

"Yes, sir, it's just ahead of me."

"Do you think we should stop the truck?"

"Sir, I know they're going to the docks and their ship is called the *Colotta*. I know there are four more women on board ship, along with enough high explosives to make a very big hole in the ground. I need to get on that ship. Let the truck go through the dock gates and let me get in there."

Bill hesitated. "This is against my best judgment, but I don't guess I've got much choice. We've contacted the Port Authority, and they said the ship does in fact belong to Rema and is scheduled to depart within the hour. It's been inspected and is clean."

"Well, they're full of shit!" Bryan's emotions were on edge. "That ship is as hot as it can be—it's smoking!"

"Calm down, Bryan," Bill responded. "I've got the Port Authority people on the line and they'll let you pass. Keep Kelly's phone with you and let us know when you think it's right for us to take the ship. We're on the way and we'll be there in fifteen minutes. Oh, and we picked up Kim—she's okay."

"That's a good thing!" Bryan replied. "These guys are nuts and they'll kill. You'd better send some people to those south warehouses—there's a guy named Jake in Warehouse B-4 who's armed, and there's a lot of high explosive in the basement of that warehouse. Tell your people to be careful of the crates marked with red dots. Oh yeah, one other thing—I stuffed a guy named Mick in a box behind B-5. He's gonna have a bad headache for a couple of days."

The truck stopped at the main security gate leading to the dock. The security guard inspected their paperwork, went back into the guard station, and returned to the truck with authorization for Ted and Maze to enter the dock area.

Bryan stopped his car just out of sight of the guard station. Looking through the trees, he could still see the truck. As soon as it moved away, Bryan pulled up and stopped beside the guard, who was still watching the truck make its way down the sloping gravel road toward the docks.

"Hi—I'm Bryan Wescott," he said, gesturing toward the truck. "I'm following that truck."

"Yes, sir, Mr. Wescott," the guard replied. "We got the word just a few minutes ago to let you through. The *Colotta* is just on the other side of the warehouse and parking lot. If you park in lot E, the ship will be right in front of you."

"Thanks." Bryan followed the guard's instructions, parking his car and making his way along the fence and the far side of the building. He stopped behind a Dumpster that sat against the building's loading dock and stared at the truck, which was only yards from his position. Maze and Ted stood in front of the truck and two men were approaching them from the warehouse.

"I'm Marvin Sales, the dock manager, and this is Robert Ryan from the customs office. I need to see your paperwork," one of them told Ted and Maze. "Robert here will inspect your container, if you'll please open it." Ted presented their documents to Marvin while Maze unlocked the container doors for the customs officer.

Bryan watched from his hidden position as Marvin shuffled the papers and Robert entered the back of the container and looked around. He could tell Ted was very uneasy.

After a few minutes, Robert emerged from the container. "Everything okay?" Maze asked.

"Looks fine to me," Robert said. Both men returned to the front of the truck, and Marvin stamped their documents. Ted took the papers from Marvin and returned them to his briefcase.

"Can we load the container now?" Ted seemed anxious to get the container on the ship.

"Well, let's see," Marvin said, looking around. "Not on this dock—we've got a union here, you know. I know the ship is scheduled to leave as soon as this container is loaded. Hang on and I'll get some help. It might take a few minutes, so just take it easy."

On the concrete dock beside the Dumpster, Bryan saw an old jacket with the name "Chuck" embroidered on it, lying next to a baseball cap and a lunchbox. He quickly put on the jacket and cap, picked up the lunchbox, and walked toward the truck. "Hey there!"

The men looked around. "Who are you?" Marvin asked.

"I'm Chuck." Bryan pointed to the name on the jacket. "I've just started working at the north warehouses and needed some OT. You Marvin? They told me to look up a guy named Marvin."

"That's me," Marvin said. "I'm glad to see you. We need all the help we can get. There are six ships ready to pull out, and I don't have nearly enough people to get the job done. These guys need to get this container loaded." He looked at Ted and Maze. "Okay, guys, pull your truck down to that white line next to the ship. Disconnect the locks on the container from the flatbed and we'll take it from there."

Maze drove the truck up to the line and started the process of uncoupling the container from the flatbed. With the briefcase in hand, Ted told him, "I'm going on board, Maze. After they get the container, park the truck and come aboard—we'll be in the front hold of the ship."

"If you don't need me any more, I'll be in the office," the customs officer informed Marvin.

"That's fine with me," Marvin replied. "Chuck and I can handle it from here."

Robert turned to leave, smiled at Bryan, and nodded. "You be careful now, you hear?" Bryan nodded back. He thought Robert knew.

"Okay, Chuck, this is what I want you to do. Wait a second!" Marvin pulled his walkie-talkie from his belt and spoke into the speaker as he looked up to the crane handler. "Jimmy, this is Chuck. I'm gonna give him the walkie-talkie and he'll direct you on the cable."

Bryan heard the reply through the radio's speaker. "Okay, boss."

"Chuck, this is what I want you to do," Marvin said, pointing to the small ladder on the container. "Climb that small ladder on the side of the container and get up on top. Jimmy will drop the cable down, and you hook it to the long bar in the middle of the container. When you get it done, hold on— Jimmy will pick the container up and move it into the ship's hold." Marvin took off his gloves and handed them to Bryan. "Take these—you'll need them to work the cable. Be careful, I don't need any injuries on my watch."

Bryan followed his instructions and climbed on top of the container. Marvin shouted up to him, "There'll be a small flatbed in the ship; line the container up and have Jimmy put the container on it. Two guys are inside the ship and they'll secure it. Disconnect the cable and Jimmy will pull it up. Climb the catwalk to get off the ship."

The container moved slowly up, over, and down into the hold of the ship as Bryan guided Jimmy to the flatbed. Just as Marvin had said, two guys locked the container down. Bryan unlocked the cable, and Jimmy pulled the cable from the ship. Bryan watched the cable as it disappeared.

"Climb down!" one of the guys on the ship's floor called to Bryan. "My name's Flipper and this here is Chris. You'd better get off the ship pretty fast—it's gonna be leaving real soon. It's a long swim from where we're going."

Bryan made his way to the catwalk and started up the metal steps. He looked behind him and saw Flipper and Chris slowly moving the container toward the front of the ship, where Ted was walking into a small office. He could see container 2150-A—the container that had held the first four women—positioned to the right and a few yards from the office. The door was open, and it appeared to be empty. Behind the office, he could make out what appeared to be a large storage cage attached to the hull of the ship; there was some movement inside, but Bryan couldn't see much else.

He made his way to the top of the catwalk and went through the ship's small door into a hallway that led to the outside of the ship. He looked around and didn't see anyone, so instead of going right toward the dock ramp, he went left toward the other side of the ship. There he found another door similar to the one he had just walked through; it read in big black letters, "Forward Hold Entrance."

He opened the door; stepped through, and found himself standing on the same catwalk he had just left. This one, however, offered him a better view of the front of the ship. In front of him were another set of metal stairs that led to the floor. He quietly eased down and through the rows of containers labeled "Tony Rema Shipping." Within a few minutes, he was on his hands and knees in the dark, hiding behind a 55-gallon oil barrel sitting several yards from the cage. He could now clearly see the four women in the cage; they were naked, handcuffed, and gagged.

Bryan saw Ted leave his small office and make his way across the ship's floor to the container he had just helped load, container 2150-B. Ted's men had unloaded it from the flatbed and set it in position beside the other container. "Okay, Chris, you and Maze go ahead and get those six women out of the container and into the cage," Ted ordered. Bryan watched as the process started.

"Hey, Ted!" Flipper called from the office. "Got a call from the captain for you."

"Be right there, Flipper—tell him it'll just be a minute. Maze, after the six women are unloaded, go ahead and finish unloading the container. Be damned careful of 25-C, the one with the four red dots."

"Boss," Maze asked, "that's the real bad one, right?"

Ted smiled. "C-4 explosive. 25 pounds of it. Oh, and bring those two gym bags and the briefcase to the office."

Maze started unloading, and Ted went to the phone to talk to the captain. After a minute or so, Ted called out, "The captain says the Port Authority has put a hold on us leaving. Something about too many ships leaving port at the same time. It's okay—it's not unusual."

Bryan knew it was time to get Bill and Peggy. He made his way back to the catwalk and found a hidden location near a porthole where he could make a phone call.

"Peggy, are you there?" he whispered into the phone.

"Yes, Bryan," Peggy replied in a calm and soft voice. "I'm here with Bill and a bunch of other people, waiting on you. Where are you?"

"I'm on board the _Colotta_, on the front catwalk overlooking the front part of the ship. There are ten naked women gagged, chained, and caged in the front of the ship behind containers 2150-A and B. Ted Darling and three other men are guarding them. They're armed with automatic weapons," he said. "I'll be behind an oil barrel across from the cage. Don't shoot me, and be very careful—there's a big box of C-4 explosive in front of container 2150-B. Give me five minutes and make it happen."

"Bryan," Peggy said, "Bill doesn't want you to move from your location." Bryan didn't respond. "Bryan? Bryan!" He turned the phone off as her voice escalated.

He retraced his steps to the oil barrel, the gun Kelly had given him drawn and ready for action. Soon, he heard a lot of commotion coming from the rear of the ship: U.S. marshals were coming down the catwalk.

In the small office, Flipper jumped up from behind the desk and grabbed his AK-47. "It's the *feds*!" he screamed, and fired at the marshals.

The marshals ducked and shouted "Put your weapons down!" as more officers entered the ship's hold. More gunfire erupted. *Rap! Rap! Rap!*

Bullets bounced off the hull just above the women, who were lying on the floor whimpering and trying to scream through their gags.

Bryan saw Flipper leave the office and run toward the back of the ship. Ted lifted his rifle and fired back toward the officers on the catwalk. A bullet struck one officer in the leg, and he went to his knees. The office windows shattered.

Suddenly, Bryan heard a man screaming at him. "You son of a bitch!" It was Chris, one of Ted's men. He jumped out from the other side of the container with an AK-47. Without hesitation, Bryan aimed his pistol and pulled the trigger. *Rap! Rap!* The bullets hit Chris in the chest with a burst of blood and his body slammed against the back of the container, his gun firing in the air. He slumped forward on his knees to lie face down in a pool of blood at Bryan's feet.

Bryan was stunned; he had never killed a man before. It all seemed unreal, like it was happening in slow motion.

Several more shots were fired, and that brought him back to reality. A second later, another body slammed against his oil barrel. It was Maze. He was dazed from the fall, sweat pouring from his face. As he looked up, Bryan swung with all his power and caught Maze on the jaw with his handgun. He slumped to the floor next to Chris.

Bryan glanced around, wondering what else was coming his way. He made eye contact with Kelly on the other side of the cage bars; somehow she had been able to push her foot out and trip Maze as he ran. As their eyes met, they shared a moment of tenderness and thankfulness.

"Who the hell are you?" Ted's voice rang out. Bryan, still on his knees, turned his head to look up at Ted. "I know you. You're the guy from the firm. Damn it! What the hell are you doing here?"

"I'm just a financial consultant." He could think of nothing else to say.

"Well, Mr. Financial Consultant, say hello to the great accountant in the sky for me." Ted had his AK-47 trained on Bryan's chest. His eyes glazed; he knew it was over.

Rap! Rap! Rap! Gunfire echoed through the ship once more. Bryan jerked at the sound. For some unknown reason, he was still breathing. Ted dropped his gun and went to his knees; the two men were face to face. Blood oozed from Ted's mouth, and his eyes rolled back in his head.

"*Whooz zee heel aar ya?*" Ted gasped as he fell forward next to the other two men.

"Mr. Nobody," Bryan said.

"You okay, Bryan?" Bill was standing there with an M-16 rifle.

"I'm not sure. A little too close for me, you know?"

Bill had a deep, distressed look on his face. "Yes, it was. Too close!"

Peggy joined the two men seconds later. "Gee, Peggy," Bryan said, smiling. "You really look cute in cameos, you know?"

"Only for you, Bryan," she responded. "Bill, we caught the other guy trying to get off the ship, and I've just been told that the captain and his crew have been arrested. The ship is secure." Several agents began freeing the women as Bryan showed Bill the cargo in the containers.

Peggy knelt down next to Kelly and helped her remove her gag. "Looks like you had a tough night."

"Peggy!" Kelly sighed. "I guess. Under different circumstances it might not have been too bad, if you know what I mean. I do need some help, though. I've got this wire around

my waist and between my legs that's absolutely cutting me in half. It's got a little buddy with it."

Peggy giggled. "Yep, let's see what we can do about that. Tell me the rest later."

They soon joined the two men in front of the container. The customs officer Robert Ryan joined them with a message for everyone to report to the downtown office as soon as possible.

"Mr. Ryan, glad to see you again," Bryan said to him.

"Nice to see you're still alive, Chuck."

"Bryan—it's Bryan, not Chuck."

"Okay, Bryan. Bill, the women are being taken to the nearest hospital for evaluation and a demolition crew is on route to disarm the torpedoes."

As they started to leave the ship, Bill searched the office Ted and his men had been using and picked up the two gym bags and the briefcase. He gave one to Bryan and he took the others. At Kelly's car, they put both gym bags in the trunk and Bill kept the briefcase.

Later, in the downtown office, the group assembled in the main conference room.

As they entered, Kim stood up. "Man, I'm glad to see you guys. Mr. Jeffers here has been telling me a little about what's going on."

"Ladies and gentlemen," Bill began as everybody gathered around the large table, "this is Mr. Greg Jeffers. He is the regional director and our boss."

"Please be seated, everybody," Mr. Jeffers said, taking the lead in the meeting. "Who would like to go first?"

"Hi, Greg," Kelly said. "I'll go first." She stood up. "As you know, over the last eighteen months, a series of young, attractive professional women were kidnapped from up and down the East Coast. Peggy and I set up shop at Bill's firm because of the new clients he was getting from overseas. These people had enough money to buy anything they wanted, and that included women.

"Our Intel told us that they were handpicking these women to become their personal property. Tonight, we found out that Tony Rema was paid a lot of money to set up the kidnappings and to transport the women to their new owners. He used Ted Darling and his men to do his dirty work.

"When Bryan and I saw Christy Wells kidnapped tonight that was the best lead we'd had. We followed them to the warehouses where they were keeping several other women caged up. That's when we found out about the gun deals Rema was doing."

"What about me?" Kim asked. "How did I get involved with this?"

"Well, Kim," Kelly said, "Rema paid a lot of money for you at the Level Three auction, and he thought he owned you. He sent Ted and his men to kidnap you, but they got Christy by mistake. You know, you two look a lot alike."

Kelly continued her report. "We found out tonight that they used the *Colotta* to transport the guns and the women, but we still don't understand how the ship was always clean when it got to port."

Bryan spoke up. "Mr. Jeffers, sir? Maybe I can shed a little light on things."

"Ah, yes, Mr. Wescott, I've heard a lot of good things about you. Please go on."

"Thank you, sir. See, after Mick took Kelly at the warehouse, I went back inside and heard Darling tell this guy Maze everything about their plans. They built the false wall in the container to hide the women and disguise the cargo. He also said that in two days, they would meet up with Tony Rema on a diesel submarine and transfer the women and the cargo from the *Colotta*. The *Colotta* would then continue to its port and would be as clean as a rug."

"A submarine?" Mr. Jeffers stood up, disturbed by what he'd just heard.

"That's right, sir. I heard Darling say that Rema bought it from Libya in a gun deal. He said that the sub anchors off a small private island near the coast of Greece, and that's where the women are taken. The island has a small airfield where the new owners can fly in and pick up their property, the women. The sub then continues to the mainland and docks in a submarine pen used by the Germans in World War II. The guns and ammo are transferred to trucks and taken to the desert for sale."

"Okay, Bryan, nice work, but what about Kelly and Christy?" Mr. Jeffers asked, a concerned look on his face.

Bryan replied, "As Ted put it, Kelly and Christy were not owned or paid for by anyone, so Rema would just sell them to one of the gun buyers in the desert."

"Thanks, Bryan," Kelly said, "just what I needed to hear."

Just then, an agent entered the room with an urgent message for Mr. Jeffers. He read the message. "I have just been notified of several leads from our friends in British Intelligence. Apparently, many of these kidnapped women are now in Greece and the surrounding area. Kelly, you and Peggy have a flight waiting as we speak. You'll meet your contact in Athens through the usual channels."

"Yes, sir," Kelly responded. "Peggy and I will leave right away."

"Bill," Mr. Jeffers said, "we need to contact the Coast Guard about this submarine and get Admiral Green on the horn. I want to speak to him myself." He looked around at the others. "Very good job tonight, people. Mr. Wescott, thank you for your work tonight; it may have saved a lot of lives. I'll be talking to you again later."

"Thank you, sir!" Bryan was very pleased.

Kelly and Peggy took Bryan by the arms and ushered him to the other side of the room. Then Kelly said quietly, "Peggy and I know that you have deep feelings for Kim, and she does love you. We think you're the right guy for her. She needs a man like you, and we know you'll do the right thing by her. Keep in touch, and keep the keys to my car—I might want it back sometime."

Bryan smiled at both women. "You watch your asses now. I must say, I've enjoyed both of you very much, and I'll never forget that. I'll take care of Kim—I do love her."

Kelly and Peggy looked at each other and said in unison, "Enjoyed both of us?" as Bryan walked off.

"Bryan!" Bill called out.

"Yes, Bill?"

"You know those two gym bags in Kelly's trunk?"

"Sure do."

"Well, if my thinking is right, it's the three million that Rema was going to invest. I guess it just got lost in the battle. It belongs to you now. Go buy that house at Pikes Point for yourself and Kim. It's our way of saying thanks."

"Time to go, Kim. You're with me now," Bryan said.

Kim turned to Bryan, and her eyes told the story. It would be a new beginning for them: much more than a master/slave relationship. "I'd say it's about time," she said.

They walked out of the office into the new day. The sun was just starting to appear in the eastern sky. He opened the car door for her and she got in.

Bryan looked up and noticed a faint breeze blowing the leaves in the oak trees next to the parking lot. "It's gonna be a great day."

The Saga Continues in "Rema's Revenge"

Follow the works of I. B. Cuffman

In the world of I. B. Cuffman, underworld BDSM fantasies of sexual conquests and sadistic tortures are unveiled in chapter after chapter. His extreme imagination takes his characters on action adventures around the globe.

1. ***Rema's Revenge***---Tony Rema, the gunrunner and kidnapper, kidnaps Bryan's lovely Kim. The adventure takes Bryan across two oceans in search of his beloved. Sex, violence, and malicious tortures confront Kim at every step.

2. ***Pirate's Bay***---Kelly and Peggy, two government agents, rescue two kidnapped women, but wind up in the clutches of a modern-day pirate and his tortures band. Bryan Wescott gets a call to go find them. His destination is an uninhabited island-Pirate's Bay.

3. ***Kinkade's Track***---Wade Kinkade is the best tracker in the county. The stagecoach is three day's overdue, and the local sheriff makes Wade a deputy. Three lovely women and a lot of money are on that stage. The women are raped and tortured by the bandits that rob the stage. Can Deputy Wade find these women, and what's it all about.

Further stories by I. B. Cuffman are in publication by R. B. Publishing. For prices and to order a copy of any of these books, write to the following address.

Rich B. Publishing
P. O. Box 404
Nichols, South Carolina
29581

E-mail--RichBPublishing@Aol.com

www.ingramcontent.com/pod-product-compliance
Lightning Source LLC
Chambersburg PA
CBHW021331070726
47496CB00016B/661